ALSO BY KOBO ABE

The Box Man

Inter Ice Age 4

The Ruined Map

The Face of Another

The Woman in the Dunes

THESE ARE BORZOI BOOKS, PUBLISHED IN NEW YORK
BY ALFRED A. KNOPF

Secret Rendezvous

SECRET
RENDEZVOUS

by Kobo Abe

Translated by Juliet W. Carpenter

Charles E. Tuttle Company
Suido 1-chome, 2–6, Bunkyo-ku, Tokyo

This edition is published by the Charles E. Tuttle Company, Inc., of Rutland, Vermont and Tokyo, Japan with editorial offices at Suido 1-chome, 2-6, Bunkyo-ku, Tokyo, Japan by special arrangement with Alfred A. Knopf, Inc., New York.

First Tuttle edition, 1981

This book is published under a continuing program designed to encourage the translation and publication of major Japanese writings not previously available in English. Conceived by the Japan Society of New York, the program is supported by the Society and the Asahi Shimbun of Tokyo.

ISBN 4-8053-0472-3
PRINTED IN JAPAN

"Love for the weak always includes a certain murderous intent."

Contents

Contents

Notebook One

Sex	Male
Name	(omitted)
Code number	M-73F
Age	32
Height	1.76 meters
Weight	59 kilograms

Thin at first glance, but muscular. Wears contact lenses for mild near-sightedness in both eyes. Slightly frizzy hair. Inconspicuous scar at left corner of mouth (from a quarrel during student days, although the subject is extremely mild-tempered). Smokes under ten cigarettes daily. Special talent is roller skating. Has worked temporarily as male nude model. Currently employed at Subaru Sporting Goods Store. Director of sales promotion for jump shoes (sporting shoes with special elastic body—air-bubble springs—built into soles). Hobby is tinkering with machines. In sixth grade, won a bronze medal in newspaper-sponsored inventor contest.

This report contains the results of an investigation of the above man. Since it is not apparently meant for publication, I won't adhere strictly to form.

Before dawn, at around ten minutes past four, as I recall, I went as scheduled to the site of the old army target practice range to take the horse his dinner, and while there was suddenly entrusted with this assignment. Since I had been about to insist that the investigation be moved into full gear anyway, I was not particularly upset. But the investigation I'd had in mind concerned the whereabouts of my wife. Unfortunately, at that point there were no indications of any kind regarding the person to be investigated, not even as to sex, and so naturally I assumed my wishes had been respected. Usually an investigation confers certain powers on the one in command; it seemed possible that at last I had won that much confidence.

Besides, the horse was in uncommonly good spirits this morning. He said he had trotted around and around the well-trodden 248-meter-long target range, managing to complete eight laps in all. During the whole time he claimed to have fallen down only three times; if true, it was quite a feat.

"In short, the trick is to run just with your two hind legs." Breathing hard between words, he wiped the sweat from his face with a towel wrapped around his neck, gulped down in a single draught the carton of milk I had brought, then stood up proudly on his hind legs and gave a little skip. "You see, I end up using my front legs, from force of habit. That's the problem right there. To run like a horse, you've got to leave all the kick up to your hind legs, and just throw in the forelegs as a kind of rudder."

We were on the impact side of the indoor target range, which stretched out on an east-west axis, long and cavernous. High along the walls at the ceiling's edge, fixed-sash skylights were lined up like train windows, but still it was quite dark. By the wall straight ahead of us were layers of sandbags, directly in front of which was a deep trench used in manipulating the targets. On either side of the trench were big lighting fixtures, also used in target practice. Their slanting rays were all that illuminated the enclosure. The west end, where the firing positions were, was like a black hole. When the horse skipped, a double shadow stretched out long and thin across the dry, white ground, like insects struggling in a spider's web.

Since the fellow was obviously convinced that he was a horse, I didn't contradict him to his face, but he was a far cry from the real thing. His balance was all off. His trunk was short and dumpy, with the hips lowered and the hind legs bent as though he were squatting over the toilet. At that rate, not even a paper saddle would have stayed put. However charitable I tried to be, at best he looked like a rickety baby camel, or a four-legged ostrich.

To make matters worse, above the waist he had on a blue tank top edged in dark red, while below the waist, in front and back, he had on navy-blue sweat pants and heavy white sneakers. Around his waist he had wrapped enough bleached cotton cloth to hide the gap between his top and his pants. It was altogether tasteless.

"Actually, now that you mention it, that's how it is with bicycles, too, isn't it? You have to apply the brakes to the rear wheel first, or going downhill it's dangerous."

"Anyway, at this rate who knows. Maybe by tomorrow I'll be able to hop around in a pair of jump shoes!"

The horse gave a short laugh; I did not join in. The echo of his laughter reverberated emptily in the air, passing by like a puff of breath. The structure of the ceiling, arches alternating with square blocks, was evidently intended to muffle sound, but it had little effect. Maybe they had built it that way to keep from using pillars.

After gulping down a ham-and-lettuce sandwich, barely chewing, the horse sipped on a cup of sugarless coffee from a thermos. He told me he wanted to stay a little longer and go on practicing. With his appearance in the founding day celebration only four days off, he seemed fairly nervous. He is evidently determined to keep his own existence a secret until then, for greater effect, but he has nothing to worry about; nobody would be crazy enough to go poking around a firing range at such an odd hour.

I was just leaving when he asked me to take charge of the investigation. Casually, he handed me a notebook and three cassette tapes. The notebook was a large one with fine-quality paper—the very notebook I am writing in now. The labels on the backs of the tapes all bore the code M-73F, with serialized numbers; he explained that they contained records of wiretapping and other means used in tracking the object of the investigation.

I couldn't help feeling suspicious. All along, with information about my wife in hand, they had been pretending to know nothing! I was enraged, and yet relieved at this evidence that somehow their plans had changed. In any case, three days had already gone by since she disappeared. It was impossible to sit still any longer. I hurried back to my room, sat down, and played the tapes through from start to finish. It took just over two hours. After listening to them all, I spent another hour or so just sitting and staring into space.

My expectations were betrayed. Nowhere in those recordings was there the slightest trace of my wife. In fact, there was no trace of any woman, let alone my wife. The one being minced, peeled, and poked at by wiretaps and shadowers was a man. A man on display, torn into fragments of tongue-clucking, throat-clearing, off-key humming, chewing, entreaties, hollow obsequious laughter, belches, sniffling, timid excuses. . . . And that man was none other than I myself, running around in frantic circles seeking my vanished wife.

Gradually, consternation gave way to indignation. Of all the asinine tricks. I could only think that I was being ridiculed. "If you want to find your wife, first find yourself"—was that what the horse was trying to say? Unfortunately, I only wanted to know where she was, nothing so very complicated. Looking for my own whereabouts would be like a pickpocket filching his own wallet, or a detective slipping handcuffs on himself. No thanks, I could do without the moralizing at this point.

On top of everything else, the horse has made me agree to some rather strange conditions. For example, to keep me from twisting facts to my own advantage, he insists that I undergo a lie detector test at any time, on demand. Also, he wants me to avoid personal pronouns as far as possible, and to write in the third person. In other words, I'm supposed to refer to myself as "the man," and to him as "the horse." Is he trying to put a gag on me, and keep me from dealing directly with anyone but himself? What is he so jittery about?

But finally, in fact, I have begun to write. Nor is this merely in grudging compliance with the horse's request. His attitude this morning contained enough genuine sincerity to satisfy me that he isn't up to any tricks. He was enthusiastic about his practicing, and when he did bring up the matter of the investigation, I was certain his expression contained sympathy. Besides, I can't overlook the fact that he used the word "incident" for the first time, thereby acknowledging my predicament, even indirectly. This curious self-investigation could be taken as just a more precise way of filing a complaint. And the directive to write in the third person might be intended to increase the credibility of the report, and attract the attention of the right people within the system—surely different ones are in charge of crime prevention, regulation, discipline, and so on. When caution is carried too far, it is all too often taken for spite.

Following instructions as closely as possible, I hope to have the semblance of a report put together by tomorrow morning. I intend to reconstruct the fragments on the tape using facts known only to me, and reproduce as faithfully as I can the conditions of the labyrinth into which this I called "he" has been driven. I do have the feeling that things which would be awkward to write about in the first person may be more manageable in the third.

Well, if this preamble seems unnecessary, I'll have no objection if it is cut out later. I leave all that to the horse's judgment.

One summer morning an ambulance suddenly drove up, although no one remembered having sent for one, and carried away the man's wife.

It was an utter bolt from the blue. Until the siren woke them up in surprise, they had both been sound asleep, and so they were caught completely unprepared. Indeed, his wife herself, the one in question, had never complained of a single symptom. But the two men who carried in the stretcher were gruff, perhaps from lack of sleep, and paid no attention: of course she wasn't ready, they said; this was an emergency, wasn't it? They both wore crested white helmets, starched white uniforms, and big gauze masks. What's more, the card they held out was accurately filled in with her name and date of birth, so it was useless to try to protest.

There was nothing to do but let matters slide for the moment. Seemingly embarrassed at her wrinkled, shrunken night-clothes, his wife lay down as directed between the two poles of the stretcher, pressing her knees together, and the two men promptly wrapped her up in a white blanket. The man and his wife never even had a chance to say good-bye.

Emitting an odor like a mixture of hair tonic and cresol, the stretcher creaked its way down the building stairs. He remembered in relief that his wife was wearing panties. Shortly thereafter the ambulance pulled away, red light flashing and double siren sounding. The man watched it off timidly through a crack in the door. Looking at his watch, he saw it was then just three minutes past four in the morning.

(The conversation below is taken from side two of tape one. The playback counter reads 729. Time is around 1:20 on the afternoon of the day in question. Place is the office of the assistant director at the hospital where the man's wife seems to have been taken. The assistant director speaks slowly in a low, un-hesitating voice; occasionally, when he says something in an undertone, his words have an ironic twist. My own voice is impatient yet expressive, and comes off rather well, I think, although I should break that habit of pursing my lips at the end of every sentence. A watch busily ticking off seconds near the mike has a jarring effect.)

ASSISTANT DIRECTOR: But what I can't understand is, why didn't you take some steps right then and there?

MAN: I did switch on the electric hot-water heater, but I guess I must have lost my head for a while.

ASSISTANT DIRECTOR: You should have gone along in the ambulance.

MAN: That's what they said over the phone at emergency, too.

ASSISTANT DIRECTOR: It only stands to reason.

MAN: But don't you think it's normal to hesitate in a situation like that?

ASSISTANT DIRECTOR: I wouldn't have hesitated for a minute myself. With very little effort an ambulance can make just as good a cover as a hearse, you know; the perfect tool for a crime. And inside that sealed room on wheels, a scantily clad young woman and two strong masked men. If it were a movie, the next scene would be pretty grim. You say your wife was dressed in thin material, crepe or something; that sort of stuff is light and comfortable in hot weather, but it's so flimsy the front would tear right off, wouldn't it?

MAN: Please, don't even say such a thing.

ASSISTANT DIRECTOR: Just a little joke. I am a realist, though, so don't expect me to swallow any story that's too far out.

MAN: But surely you know that that ambulance came to this hospital?

ASSISTANT DIRECTOR: On paper it did, yes.

MAN: Then that guard was just talking through his hat?

ASSISTANT DIRECTOR: Without proof, there's no telling.

MAN: In that case, my wife has to be here in the hospital. You see, she couldn't have gone out without a change of clothes.

Besides, at that hour only the side entrance was open, and the guard there was keeping a sharp lookout.

ASSISTANT DIRECTOR: If you want, I'll have her paged whenever you say. But really now, how could a grown woman get lost inside a hospital, in broad daylight? The police aren't going to buy a story like that.

MAN: Isn't it possible that she was forced to register by mistake?

ASSISTANT DIRECTOR: But she refused to be examined, didn't she?

MAN: Only a person connected with the hospital could have carried off anything this elaborate.

ASSISTANT DIRECTOR: All we really know for certain right now is that someone called for an ambulance.

MAN: What's that supposed to mean?

ASSISTANT DIRECTOR: If this is all true, it's a terrible disaster. I want to be of help if I possibly can, but first I have to have some substantiation. The guard is under questioning, so just leave him to us. Actually, at this point it seems to me that the question of your own innocence deserves top priority.

MAN: What are you talking about?

ASSISTANT DIRECTOR: I'm simply discussing the possibilities.

MAN: Look, I'm the victim!

ASSISTANT DIRECTOR: That doesn't necessarily mean the hospital is at fault, however.

MAN: What am I supposed to do?

ASSISTANT DIRECTOR: For now, why don't you have a talk with security? You were a little remiss in not personally checking out the scene yourself. Anyway, since you know the approximate time and place, the best thing you could do is to go back to square one and see if you can pick up any clues around the waiting room. Who knows, you might even turn up a witness or two.

(After this interview, the assistant director left the room to attend a conference, and his secretary introduced me—that is, "the man"—to the chief of security. Eventually I will give a detailed account of that meeting, but for now I will go on and copy the testimony of the guard on duty when the man's wife was admitted. Side one of the same tape. The counter reads 206. Reliability of the contents was later verified by lie detector.)

If the doctor [the assistant director] had only questioned me more fully, I was prepared to give a full account then of everything I knew. It's a shame, because in that case the entire business could probably have been straightened out before it was too late.

First I'll describe the patient's arrival at the hospital. The ambulance pulled in at 4:16 a.m., approximately thirteen minutes after a new-admission request had come from emergency center. The patient was engaged in a heated argument of some kind with the ambulance team. According to them, she had been completely docile until they stopped at the night door; then all at once she became excited, insisting that she wasn't sick, she was perfectly healthy. She wouldn't even come out of the ambulance. I went outside and tried to persuade her that she should at least let the doctor on duty have a look at her, and not try to diagnose her own case, but she wouldn't listen. As a result, I was finally forced to cancel my calls to the doctor and nurses on duty. Meanwhile the ambulance team began saying they wanted to leave, that they didn't have all night. I protested, but they said they weren't paid to cart around people who weren't even sick, and I could hardly argue with them there. Besides, Ono, the one in charge, was an old acquaintance of mine. So I put my seal on the transfer card, accepting custody of the patient—and considering how many patients get the runaround these days, shuffled from one hospital to the next, I don't think I acted altogether out of line. A return inquiry came from the nurses' station over the intercom, and I told them to cancel arrangements for the new admission. They radioed back acknowledgment.

The patient was a rather small woman . . . [he began to say "a real looker," and corrected himself] . . . very attractive, with a round face, light skin, and big, round eyes. She was dressed only in a light robe (thin cotton or synthetic fiber, pink with a pattern of black tulips), a sash (black and green net), and cotton panties (orange bikini). She carried no other belongings. I noticed from the ambulance card that her age was thirty-one, but was unable to obtain her cooperation in verifying her name and address, so I never did make sure of those.

As soon as the patient was left alone with me, she began to act extraordinarily shy, flushing red all the way down her neck. (I only mention this, by the way, in the hope that it may shed a useful sidelight on her character and appearance.) She asked if she could borrow a phone to call her husband, and I explained politely that the only phone available for outside calls was, unfortunately, the pay phone in the waiting room. Then she begged me to loan her ten yen, getting more and more upset; when her husband came, she said, he'd pay me back with a hundred or even a thousand yen. As luck would have it, though, I had nothing on me at the time but thousand-yen bills, so I couldn't help her out. When I told her half-jokingly that a coin or two might have rolled under one of the benches in the waiting room, she took me seriously and started off to have a look. I felt sorry for her then, so I loaned her a pair of slippers and told her that if she'd just wait there, her husband was bound to come eventually, but she wouldn't listen. She brushed me aside and started off again. Since I was responsible for my post there, I couldn't leave, and besides, I didn't want her to get the wrong impression, so I made no attempt to follow her.

When she didn't immediately return I assumed she might have found a ten-yen coin after all, so I buried myself in the magazine I'd been reading. As more time went by and there still wasn't any sign of her, it occurred to me that maybe the call hadn't been completely canceled for some reason, and the doctor on emergency duty had come out and run into her in the hallway. I remember feeling a sense of relief then, because I happened to have heard some gossip about that doctor, that he was quite a ladies' man. I've been asked over and over why that should have made me feel relieved, and I still can't explain it. Later, though, when I found out he had never even set foot outside the doctors' lounge that night, I regretted my hasty suspicions, and felt sincerely sorry. Concerning the patient's subsequent whereabouts, I can only say that it is all an utter mystery to me. I only know that nobody went through the side entrance again after that.

I have read through the above statement and hereby swear that the events took place exactly as recorded here, in token of which I affix my seal.

At this point let us return to the man's room. By that time the aluminum lid on the hot-water heater would have been rattling. To calm himself the man thought that he would make a cup of coffee, but search though he might, he could not find the filter paper. He was swept anew by a cold sense of loss. It was as though the ambulance had carried off not only his wife, but also, along with her, all the petty details of daily life. He sipped on plain hot water, standing up. Beads of sweat were beginning to cover his forehead, but the sharp bits of ice jabbing his stomach showed no sign of melting.

Somewhere a cat was meowing. No, that was the siren of an ambulance racing along a street hundreds of blocks away. Maybe they had finally realized their error and were coming to bring his wife back again. He opened the window. On the corrugated tin of the blinds shone a spider's web, moist with night dew. The siren stopped. The rutting cat must have found itself a new mate. At that hour, when the streets were deserted, the whole town turned into a den of mechanical cats in heat.

There was a fragrant wind, smelling like roasted beans. Must be time for the camera-film incinerators to start up. As the wind penetrated his brain, his sense of reality returned. He closed the window. Bicycle brakes squealed, and the morning paper was delivered with noiseless, rubber-soled footsteps. He felt little inclination to read it, but was unable to stop himself. First he scanned the political news on page one, then turned to the horoscope section on the back page.

High-browed; long-necked; lobes long and full; round of skull; belly full and heavy; soles thick; food, clothing, shelter adequately provided.

Suddenly it began worrying him that his wife had not taken along a change of clothes. In that condition she probably couldn't even take a taxi. About all she'd be able to do was phone him from the hospital. Surely, though, she could find somebody who would lend her the price of a phone call. Once told the ridiculous set of circumstances that had visited themselves upon her, anybody would smile benignly, take pity on her, and feel moved to generosity.

He decided to wait for her to call. While waiting, he read through the newspaper three times. Why on earth should it take so long to find ten yen? There was a photograph of a noodle shop that had burned down in a propane gas explosion. Down on the bottom right-hand corner of the same page, a tiny ad for a lost dog caught his eye.

He came to a decision. He himself would call 119, the emergency number for fires and ambulances, and see what he could find out.

Appropriately for an emergency number, someone answered before the second ring had finished.

"This is 119, emergency. Go ahead."

As the voice encouraged him, he was struck by a feeling that he had acted too soon. Feeling awkward, he softly replaced the receiver. Immediately the bell began to ring; despite himself, he backed up in consternation against the opposite wall. Plainly it was arranged so that lines were held open automatically until the caller's business had been settled. The bell rang on and on, torturing him without letup.

There was no choice but surrender. He lifted the receiver.

When he began to talk it was just as he had feared: circumstances did not lend themselves to easy explanation. It was hardly surprising if another person could not grasp an event that made no sense to him, either.

The person at the other end of the line answered patiently,

choosing his words with care. It was highly unusual, except in cases when someone had been stricken suddenly out in the street, to have a member of the family asking what hospital a patient had been admitted to. The ambulance would never set out without specific orders in the first place, and therefore it was only logical that some member of the family had to be involved. Therefore it was open to question whether a member of the family who denied having given such orders, even though the patient had in fact been accommodated, could really *be* a member of the family. He felt no obligation to give out any information. Emergency records were restricted, and no one needed to know their contents except the parties concerned, who already knew without being told.

The man was far from satisfied, but powerless to argue back. Wiping sweaty palms on his shirttail, he stretched his back and tried to collect himself. Anyway, emergency operations were evidently handled with surprising efficiency. No rush; it wasn't even six o'clock yet. His wife could still only have had contact with a few members of the night staff, at most. It wouldn't be an impossible coincidence at all if none of them had happened to have ten yen.

Besides, the sun had come out. It was a ray of light that shone only early in the morning, and even then only for a few minutes in the summertime, just lighting up the seams in the tin blinds, but a ray of light nonetheless. Darkness always makes a man fainthearted. He certainly didn't want to start a clumsy disturbance and embarrass his wife. He shaved, washed his face, and bit into a washed tomato, then inspected the contents of his briefcase and checked on the remaining number of jump shoe catalogues.

A jump shoe is a sporting shoe with a special air-bubble spring built into the undersole. Each one contains a synthetic rubber tube, sealed airtight, whose stability equals that of a good rubber ball. By riding skillfully on the bounce, it is possible to increase one's jumping range by an average of thirty-seven percent. The shoes already show signs of increasing popularity as a leisure-time game, especially among elementary and junior high students, and it is rumored that with a little market-ing ingenuity, this revolutionary product could easily develop into a new official sport.

Today he wanted to wrap up a total of at least six ac-counts, big and small. There was a current trend in office purchasing divisions, normally not too business-minded, to show surprising interest in health-improvement devices; some had even set up special "Keep the Doctor Away" booths. He chose a cheerful necktie, bright blue decorated with bunches of silver keys.

For the time being, he made up his mind to stroll down as far as the nearest fire station, which also served as ambulance dispatcher. He was still smarting from the call to emergency, and didn't expect to accomplish much there beyond easing his mind to a certain degree. When he arrived, however, the assis-tant chief, a man of chestnut-brown skin yelling exercise commands to younger men outdoors in the courtyard, turned over his role to someone else in order to apply himself fully to the man's problem. In spite of being so close geographically, they were in a different zone, he explained, and went to the phone to call the proper station for him. While they waited for the return call, he even served the man a cup of fresh hot tea.

There was indeed a record of an ambulance dispatched at 4 a.m. that morning. When the name and address the man gave matched those on record, with no further ado he was told the name of the hospital where she had been taken. After the un-fortunate beginning he had had, this time everything went al-most too smoothly. He felt like laughing out loud. Using the fire station's big map, the chief showed him the hospital's location and how to get there. It seemed too far, but when he was re-minded that conditions for accepting emergency patients had nothing to do with distance, he yielded. The time seemed too early, but he was unwilling to let this chance slip away, now that his luck had finally started to improve.

Already at 7:32, a line of fourteen or fifteen people had formed at the bus stop. He transferred from the bus to a private railway line, then to the subway, then back to another bus.

He got off the bus as directed at the stop in front of the

hospital. Down a broad lane intersecting the bus route at right angles were the hospital gates, easily recognizable. Rows of cherry trees stood arching their leafy branches, while the ground lay covered in caterpillar droppings like grape seeds. It was obviously a special lane for hospital use, seldom traveled. The gates were still shut. One side was painted black, while the other was covered with dust and reddish rust. They must be halfway through a repainting job.

There was a public phone booth on one corner of the intersection. It was then six minutes to eight, and since it appeared the gates would not be open for some time yet, he decided to try calling his office. None of the sales department staff was in. He tried calling one of the young employees who lived out in the dormitory behind the company, and caught him just as he was putting on his shoes. The man asked him to take over his morning agenda; with no idea how long it might take to track down his wife, he had little choice. The employee readily agreed, not even bothering to hear out the man's explanation. Jump shoe sales were following a sharp upward curve just then, and shoe salesmen were engaged in a frantic night-and-day scramble for customers. Having been handed a big union purchasing division scheduled for that morning by the section head himself, the young man hardly had cause for complaint.

Appropriately enough for the chosen leader of the shoes team, the man's own sales record was always far and away the best. It was commonly agreed that he had a special knack for winding up important sales. One factor might have been his skill in demonstrating the use of jump shoes for his customers. When he ran with a pair on, it was like watching the last spurt of a first-class middle-distance runner in slow motion— although he had plenty of speed, too. He could even do effortless somersaults without a flying start, like a trampoline acrobat. Since he burned up energy in proportion to his work load, he would eventually become extremely tired, but to a layman's eyes he seemed to show superhuman stamina; his reputation was accordingly excellent. And since he himself never made any claim to extraordinary powers, no fraud was involved. Merely by a display of acrobatic feats (suppressing a slight twinge of shyness), he could be confident two times out of three of bringing any deal to a safe close. There was no reason to fret over the loss of a single morning.

But whatever else happened, he did want to attend the afternoon sales conference. The company president, who had been off at a Canadian toy fair, was expected to be there. The man had finally got down on paper a plan to improve the air-bubble spring, a project he had been hard at work on for a long time, and he wanted to hand it to the president himself. He still maintained the pride and ambition he had felt as winner in the student inventor contest and hoped, if possible, to achieve some recognition for his technical skills. It could have been only imagination, but he had an idea that his present position as head of sales was due mainly to his interest in sports, and to his experience as a nude model. It was not a thought he relished. His sales record was good enough, but he was scarcely in his element now. If he could succeed in obtaining a utility model patent, he might well be able to enjoy a substantial raise in pay.

A shadow fell through the glass walls of the phone booth and merged with his.

A woman of about his age was peering inside, her body pressed close against the corner of the booth. Even when their eyes met, her gaze behind rimless glasses never wavered, exactly as if she were observing some inanimate object. She was attractively dressed in navy-blue slacks that plainly revealed the outline of her thighs, and a white blouse with a pattern of off-yellow raindrops; her spine was perfectly straight. In view of the location, he assumed that she was a nurse. He hung up the receiver and stepped outside. Holding back the door, he offered her his place.

Since she never budged from where she stood, however, they ended up standing awkwardly nose to nose. Her hair smelled like burned matches. In the slanting morning light, the lenses of her glasses were delicately tinged with color. A perspiration stain glistened in the hollow of her bosom.

"What's wrong with you?"

Addressed suddenly in a secretive whisper, the man floundered for words.

"Nothing, I'm okay...."

"Solid muscle, aren't you? I'll bet you go out for sports."

She gave his elbow a little pinch, and ran her fingers lightly along his biceps, all the way to the shoulder. For a medical examination, it was awfully provocative. Instinctively, he stepped back. But then, backed up against the wooden enclosure around one of the trees, he could retreat no farther.

The woman went on in a teasing tone.

"My, what's the matter, goose bumps? You must be here for neuralgia, or asthma. You muscular people always have trouble with your autonomic nerves. Have you got an introduction to one of the doctors?"

"I didn't come because I'm sick."

"Oh." Her voice fell, but she soon recovered. "But you know what they say—it takes a thief to catch a thief. Instead of relying on the advice of some friend, it's really safer to trust yourself to someone recommended by a professional. The cost varies according to the doctor's level, of course, but there are always young doctors who are cheap and yet tops in their fields. It's nearly hopeless trying to decide what doctor in what department is right for what illness, if you haven't got lots of experience and a backlog of trust."

As she wound up her speech, she handed the man a business card.

Founded Ten Years Ago
Emergency, outpatient, inpatient, discharge, other
All formalities carefully handled

Official Introduction Service

MANO AGENCY

Byōin-mae
8 Namiki Lane
TEL 242-2424

Suddenly a voice rang out over a portable microphone.

Parking, this way! Parking, this way!

Another portable microphone replied.

Economy hospital set! Everything the patient needs! This morning only, special sacrifice sale!

The woman bit her lower lip slightly, and gave an embarrassed laugh.

"There's a lot of competition."

On both sides of the cherry-tree-lined street, tightly packed stalls were bustling with preparations for the day. Some people were throwing open storm doors and shutters, sprinkling water around, and putting out flags; others, already set for business, had taken up position in chairs under the eaves, portable mikes in hand. They ran multiservice agencies, with signs that advertised expert troubleshooting.

"I'm really fine. I don't plan to be examined or anything."

"It doesn't have to be for a medical examination, you know. We help with any kind of problem."

"I can take care of it one way or another myself."

"Just the other day we found a buyer for a wholesale dealer in magnetic chessboards that you play on in bed, and he was delighted. And we made all the arrangements for a TV man who wanted to photograph the expressions on people's faces in their dying moments. . . ."

"All I want is to go to the night reception desk or whatever it's called, you know, the place where they admit emergency patients, and check out a couple of things with whoever's in charge there."

"You don't seem to be a newspaper reporter. . . ."

"Nope."

"You say you just want to check out a few things, but it isn't that easy. They have a reputation for strictness over there. Only ambulances can go in. They can't make any exceptions, because once they bend the rules, all sorts of tramps and drunks start making up excuses to sneak in."

"If I walk right in through the front door, and go through all the proper procedures . . ."

"There, that's why amateurs are no good. The front desk opens at nine. The new shift comes on at eight, and by eight-thirty the old shift has all gone home, so how are you going to get there in time?"

"What time is it now?"

"Two minutes after eight."

"Damn."

"See, I told you: 'It takes a thief . . .' Registration fee is seven hundred eighty yen. That's an agreed charge so I can't mark it down for you, but let's see, if everything goes all right I can hold the total cost, including a small remuneration for the other party, down to twenty-five hundred yen."

(It appears that I've gotten unnecessarily hung up on this scene in front of the phone booth, which in terms of the investigation of myself is not all that important. And if use of the first person here offends, it's fine with me if this part is rewritten in the third person. Actually, the tapes I received from the horse start here. It makes no sense to me why already, at this point, before I had even introduced myself to anyone in the hospital, they should have been keeping tabs on me with hidden microphones. The only conclusion I can draw is that my wife's disappearance must have been planned all along. I mean to confront the horse with this point tomorrow morning.)

The woman's store was the seventh one down, on the same side of the street as the phone booth. Half the store was taken up by the show window, where various sample wares reading "Get Well Soon," "Congratulations on Your Recovery," and the like were displayed with their price tags. The rolled-up mat leaning against the wall by the sliding door was probably there to keep out the afternoon sun. The inside of the store was dark; behind a counter partitioning off one side was a bald little man with a beard.

"Here's a customer!" the woman called over briskly to the

beard. "Take care of the fee, will you?" With a wink at the man, she disappeared into a back room behind a door half-covered with a large swimsuit calendar.

The beard brought out a piece of paper from under the counter and invited the man to be seated.

"Looks like another hot one, doesn't it?"

"How much was it again?"

"Seven hundred, and uh, eighty. . . ."

The beard put the hundred-yen coins in a portable cash-box, and tossed the remaining ten-yen coins into the mouth of a beckoning-cat figurine about thirty centimeters tall. He stamped a rubber seal on a token receipt, and handed it over. Then, sliding his hips forward, he slouched back in his chair and gazed out absently at the street with eyes like empty holes. Holding his hands to his chest, fingertips touching, he began rapidly moving his fingers. Suddenly, between two fingers appeared a ten-yen coin. It spun around and split in two. Immediately the two joined back into one, only to divide then into three. The changes were swift, his fingerwork so skillful that it was impossible to say whether he had succeeded in making one coin look like three, or three like one.

"You're too good to be an amateur."

"I'm not. I'm professional, but nowadays magic tricks are all the rage. Nobody cares about sleight of hand any more."

"Are they different, then, magic tricks and sleight of hand?"

"Sleight of hand is an art, but magic tricks are just a gimmick." The coins disappeared from between his fingers. "Tell me, have you got venereal disease?"

"Why?"

"People who don't like to say what they're here for almost always have V.D."

"I'm not sick."

An expectant stir went through the rows of cherry trees, as though a rare breeze might soon appear. At the store across the street, the voice over the portable microphone went up in volume.

For clothes to rent, come to Sakura Supply! Fit, color,

*style, we have it all at Sakura Supply. Women's clothing in-
cludes one free accessory. Sakura Supply takes pride in its large
inventory, experience and reliability. Reasonable deposits. Half-
price to any licensed driver. Seeing is believing! Come to Sakura
Supply for clothes to rent. . . .*

"That's right—I've got to rent some clothes!"

The man started up from his seat. His attention concentrated on finding his wife, he had forgotten all about the vital
need for a change of clothes for her.

"A take-out, eh?"

The beard punched his right fist into his left palm like a
conspirator.

"Take-out?"

Instead of explaining, the beard brought out a big album
on top of the counter and began rattling on at great speed.

"Age, size, favorite color . . . oh, more or less will do. If
you know her approximate height, then you can get by with
'free' size, unlike with men's clothes."

"She's about one hundred sixty centimeters, and she's
about standard build, I guess."

The beard thumbed quickly through the album pages. A
thin-legged model wearing a sleeveless dress smiled, puckering
up pink lips. The dress was of some light material, loosely
pleated from the top down, with a belt tied around the waist to
give a full, baggy effect. If the shade of beige had not been
bright and cheerful, the design might have seemed a trifle
archaic.

"How about something along these lines? You can adjust
the length with the belt, and it folds up small enough to fit in
your pocket. We always recommend it for take-outs. And while
you're at it, how about a ring, a necklace, or a pair of sun-
glasses? Just one little touch like that makes rented clothes look
so natural they seem like your own."

The woman returned from the back room, where she had
been haggling over the phone with the night guard; evidently he
had been about to go home. It had been nip-and-tuck, but
finally she had negotiated an agreement. Her fee, including
a deposit on the clothes, came to 15,500 yen. That left only

1,230 yen in the man's wallet. While they settled the bill, the beard wrapped up the dress. With a little effort it fit inside the man's pocket, just as advertised. They were supposed to have included some sort of free accessory, but he was hurried outside without a chance to look and see what it was.

To get to the night entrance, she told him, turn left by the front gate and follow along the wall for about three hundred meters. She gave him simple instructions for speaking to the guard, then ran her fingers up his side while she hurried him off in a suggestive whisper.

"Run along now, and if there's ever anything else, just give me a call, any time."

The man ran off under the arching cherry branches. He was positive that even now, if he tried, he could still do a hundred meters in less than thirteen seconds.

There was an open space at a break in the wall, and a sloping concrete driveway with ridges to prevent skidding. The door he sought lay beyond. A cylindrical object sticking out at an angle beside the red door light was doubtless that TV surveillance camera. Following instructions, he pushed the black button just below the red ambulance button, and a voice came out over the intercom. He gave his receipt number from the Mano Agency, and the door opened. Must be a remote-control automatic door. Empty, gray space stuck against his face like cold, wet paper.

As his eyes became accustomed to the light, the drab gray color turned into a pure white waiting room. The room was not very large, presumably because it was used only for emergency cases; a bed on wheels took up almost one quarter of the space. The floor was tiled, as in operating rooms, and the lights on the ceiling overhead were movable. It might have been designed to double as an emergency treatment room if needed. Across from the emergency entrance was the reception desk, and directly on its right were two doors. The farther one was stainless steel. The wall at right angles to it was occupied entirely by the wide doors of a freight elevator. Except for the stainless-steel door, everything was white, including the frame around the reception desk window and even the curtain pulled across the other side of the glass.

The man shrank before so much whiteness. The impersonality of the color had the violent effect of freezing all emotion. It seemed as though his wife had slipped even farther away.

The curtain moved. The glass window slid sideways half the width of one pane, and the pasty face of an old man appeared, eyes upturned. At his blank, languid expression, the man's hopes fell again.

There was no need to introduce himself, however. The guard seemed to know all about his purpose in coming. That was a good sign; it was proof that his wife had been there. A sudden relaxation of the joints in his body made him realize how intense the worry and strain had been.

The payoff from the Mano Agency must have done its work; once the old codger opened his mouth he was surprisingly talkative. Doubtless he had seemed languid before only because he had been busy thinking. He had a habit of moistening his upper lip as he spoke. In the brief glimpses thus afforded, the tip of his tongue appeared unnaturally red. Maybe the age spots around his cheekbones and the white hair made him seem older than he really was.

Anyway, he talked too much. What the devil was he going on and on for, when all the man needed to know was where his wife was? It was like purposely stirring sediment into a jar to muddy the water. Anxiety rose up in him again.

(The counter is at 68; after the exchange with the woman from the Mano Agency in front of the public telephone, the hidden microphone was shut off for a while, and starts up again around here. The mike and recording technique are both different from before, and as a result there is a considerable change in sound quality.

Of the scenes beginning at 68, those explaining how she refused to be examined and went off to the outpatient waiting room to look for a ten-yen coin have already been covered in detail in the guard's statement above—counter number 206—so I will omit them here. Next I will try to organize the data concerning my wife's mysterious vanishing act, relying mainly on the guard's explanation. In part, I have made some additions based on inference and on knowledge acquired later.)

The guard was thrown into confusion. If the man had not come around asking questions, he could very likely have gone on pretending that nothing had ever happened,

At 8:18, when he received the inquiry from the Mano Agency, the guard had just returned to his room, having completed the eight o'clock transfer to the next shift. The change of shift usually took place in certain steps, as follows. First he would look in the mirror and comb his hair, counting the number of hairs that fell out, and straighten the collar of his uniform; a guard's uniform consists of a white jacket with black trim on the collar, so when the collar is twisted it is especially noticeable. Then he would make sure that his bunch of keys was in order, and leave by the door opposite the emergency exit, going down a narrow corridor to the outpatient waiting room.

The waiting room was large and spacious, as big as a tennis court. Viewed from the front entrance, the pharmacy and cashier were on the right, with various reception windows lined up on the left. Straight ahead was a five-meter-wide opening, leading to examining rooms and doctors' offices, that was shut off by steel fire doors. The pharmacy counter was equipped with an electrical signboard to announce the numbers of prescriptions ready to be picked up. Four rows of nine benches facing that board were the room's main fixtures, occupying the better part of its space. Built into the lower left-hand corner of the fire doors was a small, waist-high door, from beyond which could be heard the voices of cleaning women on the day shift as roll was called.

At eight o'clock a buzzer would go off, sounding the five-minute warning. Taking a quick look around the waiting room, the guard would then unlock the small door. His replacement on the day shift would duck down and walk through. The new man's uniform, a white jacket with black trim on the collar, was identical to that of the night guard. The two men would exchange perfunctory greetings. The night guard would hand over the bunch of keys. If there were any incidents to report, he would do so either orally or in written form.

About that time, the pharmacists and office workers would start reporting to work one by one. They, however, would come down directly from the second floor, where the employees' lockers were located (since the building was constructed on a hill, the employees' entrance was on the second floor, too), using a stairway that connected to the work area. Therefore, even after the areas behind the reception windows were bustling with activity, the waiting room itself remained silent. The two men would take a turn together around the room. It was a mere ritual, with no further meaning; that done, the change of shift was accomplished. The day guard would proceed to unlock the visitors' lavatory and the utility closet, and signal through the small doorway. Then the five cleaning women would pour in, chattering loudly and cheerfully among themselves, and the new day would be under way. The day guard would head for his room by the front entrance, and the night guard would be free to leave.

But on this particular morning, things had been a little different. There was that female patient brought in by ambulance. When he stopped to think about it, nearly four hours had gone by; it was a long time since she had gone into the outpatient waiting room to look for a ten-yen coin. No one had come for her. He had an uneasy feeling; it was an irritating sensation, like a smoldering ashtray. Yet for some reason he refrained from going to check up on her. No sense in worrying over nothing, he told himself; probably she got tired while looking for a coin, and dozed off on one of the benches when she sat down to rest. Before the next shift came on, it would be a good idea to find her a change of clothes so that she could leave by the side entrance. It should be possible to negotiate with some agency and have them take care of it on a pay-later basis.

In the end, however, the thing he feared most had actually

come to pass: the woman had vanished into thin air. Since the entire room could be seen at a glance, it was pointless to search, but for form's sake he peered diligently in every corner, behind pillars, in hollows in the walls, and under all the benches. Knowing it was useless, he tried all the doors leading into the waiting room from the pharmacy, the cashier's office, and the reception areas. All were securely locked from the inside.

Well, now he was stuck with a messy problem. How could he ever report this to the satisfaction of the day guard? During the night the outpatient waiting room turned into a cul-de-sac, the hall leading to the emergency entrance its one and only outlet. It was a veritable "sealed room," of the kind so popular in mystery novels. Of course, the guard had made his own deductions already—even this sealed room was not completely without a loophole. But she couldn't have done it alone; someone must have helped her. The doors were all constructed in such a way that from the inside they opened with a mere turn of the knob, although from the waiting room they opened only with a key.

Who could possibly have done such a thing? He was not without some idea, but the trouble was, it amounted to nothing but suspicion. And even if his surmise were correct, the fellow was dangerous. Any attempt to incriminate him would only get himself into hot water. Still and all, he could not just report the woman's disappearance as an ordinary fact. It was deliberately inviting them to assume that he had been asleep on the job. The only thing to do, then, was to act as if nothing out of the ordinary had ever happened.

The guard made up his mind. He decided to say nothing at all about the woman.

No sooner had he settled on this course of action, however, than he learned from the Mano Agency of the man's arrival. Worse luck. No need to ask what his business was. It had to be about that woman. He would have preferred not to see him but if he refused, that would only send the fellow automatically over into the province of the day guard, which would be even worse. That would expose the fact that he had lied in his report. Failure to report dutifully was a serious offense. Why should he lose his job over someone else's affairs? Anyway, there seemed to be no choice but to go ahead and see him. Besides, if this guy was dumb enough to let his wife get stolen in the first place, maybe he could still fast-talk his way out of it somehow.

(Below is a copy of the last line in the emergency reception ledger.)

	1977	a.m.		yes					TEL( )
6	8	4:16	cloudy		Emer.	31	F	Family; other; address	
	29	p.m.		no					

"Isn't this the one you're looking for?"

The guard spoke in a gravelly voice, not surprising for someone just coming off the night shift, as he slid the hardbound register book across the counter. On the last line of the page it lay opened to was a half-completed entry with two red-ink lines drawn through in evident sign of cancellation.

"Well, the age matches, and the time of arrival seems about right."

"Then I can't be much help. As you can plainly see, the name and address are blank. She wasn't ever formally admitted."

"But she hasn't come back. It doesn't make any sense, does it? If you'll just tell me where to look, I'll go try to find her myself."

"The only place to look is right here, I'm afraid."

"Here?"

Faint waves of tension showed in the man's posture and gaze. The guard gave an uncomfortable half-smile. His two false front teeth were unnaturally white.

"What I mean is, if she isn't here then there's no point in looking anyplace else, that's all."

"Is she here?"

"See for yourself."

The guard moved aside to give the man a clear view. Inside was a simple room about three and a half meters square, with shallow shelves and a desk. There was no space where anybody could have hidden.

"But she can't have gone outside again dressed like that."

"No, not dressed like that."

"Should I report it to the police?"

"I wouldn't if I were you. That's only going to make matters worse. Any woman thirty-one years old is big enough to take care of herself, and then some. If you raise a fuss, you're only going to make a spectacle of yourself."

"But you can't expect me to believe a story like that, as if a rabbit had just vanished inside a hat. . . ."

"Every trick has some kind of gimmick, that's for sure."

"Where does that elevator go?"

The man's quick eyes brought the rear elevator within range of action. The guard was just as fast. Lunging out the door, he blocked the man's way and looked him critically up and down.

"Don't give up easy, do you? All right, then, I'll tell you; it goes direct to the third floor. The doctors' lounge is up there, and the nurses' station and emergency operating rooms, stuff like that. Nobody goes up but emergency patients with admission cards, and nobody comes down but certified dead bodies. . . . Your wife couldn't have been on this elevator, mister, because she wasn't either one yet."

"Then where is she?"

The guard turned and opened the stainless-steel door. It was smooth and heavy. An invisible stream of cold air poured out around their feet.

"This is the morgue, where they keep the bodies in cold storage. When it's empty we use it to chill our beer. Comes in handy. Some of the guys go ahead and use it even when there's a stiff in there, but not me. I only use it when the sign says 'Vacant.' "

He brought out a bottle of beer, applied it to the edge of the door handle, and expertly pried off the cap. It barely foamed at all, no doubt because it was chilled. He stuck an arm in behind the reception window and took out a teacup, gave its rim a wipe with his finger, and poured in some of the contents of the bottle.

"I wish you wouldn't dodge the question."

The guard gulped down one cupful and poured out a second, mumbling in a flat, subdued voice, "You want me to take down your phone number? If I find anything out I'll let you know right away."

The man stared silently at the guard's hands. He kept staring, not moving a muscle, until the bottle was completely empty.

At last the guard seemed to break down. He wiped away drops of sweat and gave a sigh, as though he were the loser in a game of endurance, beaten by the man's surprising obstinacy, and there was nothing to do but concede defeat. Tracing bubbles in the bottom of the teacup with his eyes, in a secretive voice he finally began to open up and talk.

In order to prove for himself just how impossible it was to escape at night from the outpatient waiting room, where his wife had last been heard from, the man ought to go right over and make an on-the-spot investigation. Unfortunately, the day guard had already come on duty, and the cleaning women had started their operations; if he poked his head in now and gave them a chance to remember what he looked like, that would only cause trouble for any later strategy. The key to success lay in doing everything as discreetly as possible. Right now the best thing to do was trust him, the guard, and take his word for it that the rabbit had in fact been cornered in a silk hat with no way out.

Her disappearance was by no means a mere coincidence or accident of some kind, as the man assumed. There was positively no way to get out of that sealed room without the help of an accomplice. That would no doubt be a hard point for him to swallow, but there was nothing to do but face the facts bravely, head on.

Even assuming that there has been an accomplice, though, who could it have been? The first possibility that suggested itself —he hesitated to say this in front of the man—was none other than the young doctor on emergency-call duty that night. Of course, the ward doctors and other hospital employees were not above suspicion either, for that matter, but for the very reason that there were so many of them, it would have been difficult to escape the watchful eyes of nurses and others. Besides, before arriving at the outpatient building, anyone attempting such a thing would have had to go down long corridors and cross under the lights in the garden; even if such a person had been wearing a white uniform, assurance of safe conduct, any patrolman in the vicinity would surely have taken note of such suspicious behavior. On the other hand, the doctor on emergency duty could safely move around unaccompanied, and since he had a master key to the second-floor locker room, he could go unseen from the third-floor lounge down to the waiting room any time. Those were ideal conditions for leading her around. Besides, there was considerable gossip about what went on between that surgeon and the nurses; he was still single, even if his hair was horribly greasy. No matter how you looked at it, it had to have been a deliberate, prearranged rendezvous. Even so, it was going pretty far to call out an ambulance just to indulge in a little hanky-panky. He must have had the hots so bad it had gone to his head.

"Do you mean to say that with all those suspicions, you just stood by and let the whole thing happen right under your very nose?"

"Like it or not, the guy's a doctor."

"What's that got to do with it?"

"Nobody wants to have the wrong thing put down on their chart in the patient evaluation space, right?"

"That's got nothing to do with me. I've never had more than a cold or the measles in my life."

"You've got plenty of guts."

"Tell me his number and I'll call him up myself."

"The phone's no good. What kind of an idiot would confess to anything over the telephone? You've got to go straight to the scene of the crime and get hold of some hard proof. If you really mean business, I'll give you a hand. I'll show you the way to the doctors' lounge if you follow me carefully. The doctor leaves there at nine. But let's get one thing straight: I don't want to get mixed up in this any more than I already am. It might surprise you to find this out, but as a matter of fact I'm a model patient. A kind of trusty. Now that I've got myself a good job, I don't want anything to mess it up."

It was an odd elevator, skipping the second floor and stopping only at the third. It moved at a crawl, but made an enormous racket. The odor of antiseptic solution stung their nostrils.

He learned from the guard how to behave inconspicuously inside the hospital. His ordinary street clothes were no problem, but since they meant he had to be either a sickbed visitor or a dealer of some kind, they put certain restrictions on his range of actions and on the time period in which he could afford to be seen. The safest course would be to wear a white coat. There were subtle distinctions in the types worn by doctors, technicians, office workers, and so on; ultimately they broke down into over a dozen different categories. Of course, that made them all the harder to get hold of; you needed a hospital identity card to buy one from the main store. Next best was to dress like a patient or a custodian. Patients had no fixed style of dress; they could wear a nightgown or pajamas or anything suitable for wearing in bed. (In that sense, his wife had been dressed in the most inconspicuous way possible. However, few patients were normally up and about during the hours from eight till ten in the morning.) A custodian naturally had to wear something immediately identifiable as work clothes.

All he could do for the time being was take off his suit coat, loosen his necktie, and try to look as comfortable as possible, hoping that he fell somewhere between a lab technician who had soiled his uniform and a custodian who had torn his work clothes. Then he remembered the sample pair of jump shoes in his briefcase, and suggested changing out of his leather shoes into them; except for their thicker soles, they were just like ordinary sneakers. The guard agreed. That gave him a much more casual look.

They got off the elevator to find themselves near one end of a corridor. On the end wall hung a conspicuous sign, white with orange lettering, that said NIGHT ENTRANCE, with an arrow pointing down. Turning around, they saw aluminum-framed windows at evenly spaced intervals on the right; even though sunlight did not shine in directly from outdoors, the entire corridor was a tube of light. On the left, black shadows were carved out by matching sets of swinging double doors, transom windows along the wainscot, and an indentation that seemed to be a stairwell. They came to some kind of laboratory room. Next was the nurses' station, which despite the sight of people busily at work was as quiet as a silent movie. The man instinctively softened his footsteps. Fortunately, jump shoes make almost no noise. Moving past the nurses' station, they came to the first stairway.

The stairway consisted of a mere four steps, apparently connecting to a newer wing which had been added on at a different level. Another corridor veered off at an angle. Poorly lit and narrow, it was blocked by a wood-framed vinyl screen, beyond which there seemed to be a temporary data storage room or something of the sort. A door on this side of the screen was marked AUTHORIZED PERSONNEL ONLY, the words circled in red for emphasis. The two men slipped through the door and came out into another corridor that was a sudden dazzling white, like the first.

A stairway and an elevator stood side by side. Somehow they had arrived on the second floor. Passing in front of an unmarked door, a doorless utility room, and a lavatory, finally they came to a small smoking lounge that was crowded with three wooden benches, a metal ashtray, and two vending machines, one for cigarettes and one for coffee. A wheelchair with a loose wheel stood to one side. The hall divided there, one side turning right and the other slanting left at an angle. There were two signboards: one, green with white lettering, said NUMBER THREE CONSULTATION and pointed to the right, while the other, in black on orange, said OUTPATIENT DUTY and pointed back the way they had come. The slanting left-hand corridor had no sign.

The unmarked corridor must also have been built at a different time, since there was a slight grade in its juncture with the main corridor. Everywhere else the ubiquitous white shone like plastic, but there it was the color of cheap paint. The floor, too, changed to wood planks; utter silence gave the hall a dismal cast, while sporadic windows made it resemble the gray-and-white underbelly of a snake.

The on-duty doctors' lounge was inside that snake belly, he was told. Since the corridor came to a dead end, the doctor would have to pass by this smoking lounge in order to get wherever he was going. At last, having come this far, the guard seemed to become ill at ease. In parting, he said that he hated to repeat himself, but he didn't want to get mixed up in this business any further, so why not call it quits right there. Then, scratching furiously behind one ear, he tore off down the hall with the green sign.

The time was 8:43. When the man sat down on a bench, his sweat-soaked trousers stuck to his thighs. He felt like urinating, but decided to hold off in fear of missing the doctor. He was only more likely to attract attention by sitting there doing nothing, though, so he put one hundred yen in the slot for a cup of coffee and sat down to sip it slowly, buying time. He was impressed by the intricacy of the way they had come, and strongly doubted his ability to make it back alone. A young nurse ran by from the green sign toward the orange one, scuffling her feet along the floor as she carried some sort of steaming wide-mouthed jar. A muttering mechanical noise beat ceaselessly against the floor; a tall, wheeled cage containing aluminum breakfast trays scraped against the ceiling as it went by. For a few seconds he thought he heard from somewhere a woman's stifled sobbing.

When the paper cup was half empty, there came the sound of a door opening and closing down the unmarked corridor. Shuffling footsteps came closer over the wood-planked floor. It was a doctor, of such fine, strapping physique that his white coat seemed too short for him. He walked with chin high and chest thrust out, as smoothly as if he were gliding on rails. His black, wide-rimmed spectacles had thick lenses.

Since there seemed to be only one doctor on emergency call, this had to be the one. Had this guy really taken my wife and hidden her somewhere? Or rather, had she actually given in to his enticing and acted out that stagy abduction? I put every memory that came to mind through a compressor, squeezing as hard as I could to see if my wife's behavior had ever contained anything to arouse the slightest suspicion. The liquid I extracted was clear and pure. Had ever a man been so brilliantly taken in? I was disgusted with myself. Suddenly the other man's figure was garishly intensified, like a TV picture whose color control had gone wrong.

It wasn't that I was afraid. Even granting that the doctor had an intimidating way about him, I have confidence in my own strength. I tend to look thinner in my clothes than I really am, so it's hard to tell from the outside, but I'm in pretty good shape, if I do say so. A little difference in weight wouldn't throw me. It wasn't that I shrank back—I was purposely holding myself back. I didn't want to give in to my emotions and ruin the opportunity. That may sound like bluffing, but don't forget, I used to be a nude model. The first time I was asked, they said it was for a medical/sports magazine, so I let myself be talked into it. I quit as soon as I found out they were selling to fag magazines. That gave me the chance for the job I have now at the sporting goods store, so I can't complain, but it's nothing I like to brag about. Although according to that photographer, they're pretty strict in their requirements for models for those fag magazines. They don't want anyone who's too tough, but if you look too namby-pamby, that's even worse. Apparently the essential quality is an agile, quick aggressiveness.

I guess I've wandered pretty far off the track. Worse than that, I forgot and started writing in the first person. But bear in mind, I had all I could do at that moment to maintain my equilibrium. Right now I am listening to the sound of those footsteps again over the playback machine. The counter reads

874. The shoes he was wearing were low, slipper-style ones with thin leather soles, so the volume is not too loud, but even so, the sound seems extraordinarily distinct. It must be partly because I was sitting so still on the bench. That noise in the background like shallow waves breaking on a beach is the sound of my own breathing. The footsteps grow plainer and plainer, until they are so close that I can almost tell his exact mannerisms of gait, and even how far down the soles of his shoes had worn. Finally, just on the verge of colliding with the microphone, the footsteps recede and are lost again in the surrounding noise. There ends the first side of the first tape. I rewind it back to 874 on the dial, flick the switch to playback, and again the footsteps come closer. Time after time, again and again, they keep coming closer.

This is one peculiar job I have taken on. No matter how I follow myself around, I will never see anything but my own backside, when what I want to know about lies beyond: the empty space, for example, that I never knew or dreamed existed until it was invaded by that doctor's footsteps . . . the space that ever since has grown endlessly wider, separating my wife and me . . . the ground that anyone can walk around on freely, that belongs to nobody . . . the jealousy like a bed of hard, frozen lava, leaving only the imprint of anger. . . .

The doctor never glanced toward the man. Turning left at the smoking lounge, he headed in the direction of the green sign— the same way that the guard had gone. Staring into space from behind his thick glasses, eyes half closed, he passed by without altering his posture or his gait. The man tossed the rest of his coffee into the ashtray, paper cup and all, and stood up. He waited until a good fifteen meters lay between them before starting to follow.

At the first corner was an elevator. The doors opened as soon as the doctor pushed the button; evidently it had been waiting right there. The doctor went inside. It seemed impossible to make it there in time. Afraid he had lost him already, the man began to run. Thanks to the jump shoes, he bounded seven or eight centimeters into the air and lurched forward as he sprinted. Not surprisingly, he attracted the attention of the doctor, who pressed the "Doors Open" button and held the elevator for him. Nothing is so awkward as a demonstration of humanity by the enemy. The man bowed his head without speaking, and the doctor followed suit, staring wordlessly at the man's feet.

The doctor had pushed the fifth-floor button; pretending not to have seen, the man pushed the same one. The numbers went up to seven. Was the doctor on some errand of unfinished business in the hospital? Or was there somewhere on the fifth floor a private room that he used for his secret rendezvous?

They stepped out into a lobby that was plain but cheerful and clean, with a revolving door. The man could hardly believe his eyes, but there just beyond the door was the ground. Not the artificial ground made by piling dirt on terraces and roof gardens, either, but the real thing: you could have dug down clear to the center of the earth. Beyond the entranceway was a street, not too wide, but fitted with a sidewalk and planted with trees. Coming from the building's front entrance this was the fifth floor, but evidently on this side it was ground level. The building must be constructed on a fairly steep hill.

There was neither receptionist nor guard. Unchallenged by anyone, he followed the doctor outside. In the sudden heat his neck seemed to swell. The sky was blue only at the zenith, turning a murky gray toward the horizon. Looked like another bad day of smog. A microbus drove past and discharged a load of men and women in white onto the pavement. If they were running an intrahospital shuttle bus, this must be a hell of a big place.

The street, however, seemed fairly ordinary. A few buildings were obviously hospital annexes or laboratories, but side by side with those were camera stores and groceries of the kind you might see anywhere. Depending on your point of view, either the street area was working its way into the hospital or the hospital was spilling out into the streets. The first intersection had an overpass, and the wide, two-lane thoroughfare below was already bumper to bumper with cars heading both ways. That must have been the main highway before the hospital was enlarged across those two hills. He was unable to decide whether the tall, glass-plated building on one corner of the intersection belonged to the street or to the hospital, until finally he made out the quiet lettering in windows on the top floor: BEDDING FOR RENT. Of course; catering to a big hospital like this, a bedding rental service would do a good business. So maybe this was part of the hospital grounds after all.

Next they came to a three-way intersection with a traffic light. One way led steeply downhill, with a small diner two doors from the corner. The doctor disappeared inside as if it were a familiar haunt. Instead of a sign, a big fork stuck out from under the eaves; spaghetti seemed to be the house specialty. For a clandestine meeting place it was certainly discreet enough. The man calmed his breathing and stretched the kinks out of his arm and leg muscles, preparing himself to rush in at a moment's notice. It must have been still too early; besides the doctor, there was no sign of anyone, let alone the man's wife. A sign announced that today's special was cod roe rice balls with soup, 370 yen; a bargain, all right, but he'd hold off. The doctor was wiping his face with a cold towel, menu in one hand, so he was probably still unaware of the man's presence. The man decided to go on past and keep watch from the corner, by the alley at the bottom of the hill. He was puzzled by this turn of events. This was strange behavior from someone who had gone to all the trouble of sending out an ambulance in order to abduct a woman. Or was she supposed to show up here later? Either way, he thought, he would be in a good position.

His hunger was still bearable, but the strain on his bladder had slowly reached the breaking point. He started to piss beside a straw-mat store that was still closed. Even now there was little foot traffic, this being within hospital territory. All at once, around the alley corner came a pair of young men in sweat pants. With their close-cropped hair and identical mustaches, they looked rather like members of a student karate club. Evidently they had been running fairly hard; their bodies were wrapped in a membrane of perspiration. As they went by, one of them jabbed the man sharply in the side. His flow of urine stopped. Hurriedly he zipped up his fly. A dribble of urine formed a stain on his trousers, enough to show. Much to his relief, the pair ran on past. Had he not been taking a leak just then, he would hardly have let the incident pass in silence. That was a close call; he came damn near making a scene and ruining everything.

He lit a cigarette. Around his sharply pricked ears time flew past like a gust of wind, but in his abdomen it lay accumulating in a leaden, unmoving mass. Before he knew it, four cigarette butts lay scattered at his feet, crushed and split open, and the fifth was between his lips. He had used up half his day's allotment. He would have to be extra careful with the rest.

When he had smoked the fifth cigarette down about two centimeters, the doctor emerged from the restaurant, showing no sign of either irritability or disappointment. Then it had not been an assignation after all. The man's conviction began to waver; if he stopped tailing him now, though, that meant the one ray of hope he had clung to would be cut off. The doctor had removed his white coat; that would account for the bulge in his briefcase. Or could it be leftover spaghetti that he was taking to the man's wife?

The doctor went back to the three-way intersection and turned left, coming to a subway station. Since there was a thin trickle of people going in and out, the man followed behind without hesitation. The doctor walked straight past the ticket gate, through the underpass, and out the other side. The scenery there was completely different; it was a narrow, deserted road overlooking a cliff, with ragweed as tall as a man's head growing at the roadside. From an overhead tunnel parallel with the road, a set of tracks cut into the hillside. Perhaps it was not a subway after all, then. He wanted to check and make sure, but there were no station signs on that side.

The road was straight. Bad luck if the doctor should happen to glance around, but fortunately he appeared oblivious to his surroundings. He seemed full of confidence, or perhaps he was just busy thinking. Through the ragweed leaves, a gray sea spread out before their eyes. Along the quay, yellow-ocher buildings made a line of stripes that swayed, burning, in the August sun. If those should happen to be warehouses of a certain rubber company, then the man thought he might have some idea where he was.

As they went down a flight of steep hewn-stone stairs, a shop-lined street came into view about halfway down the hill. The cliff ledge protruded out like a canopy, making it invisible from above. One in every five stores was a flower or fruit shop, giving the area a festive look even though business seemed slow. The bulk of trade here, too, must be with the hospital. Midway down the street was a tunnel leading back up to high ground. At the entrance stood a stone statue of Jizō, guardian of children, with a plastic orchid stuck in either ear; water pouring from a drain made a bubbling pool at his feet. The far end of the tunnel was provided with stairs. Climbing up to the top, they came out into an open residential section.

Poorly kept lawns and sparsely planted trees covered the hill, with identical houses scattered here and there. The hill's convex shape made visibility poor, but as nearly as he could judge, there were a good twenty or thirty of the structures. All were two-storied, with a central entrance shared by two households, right and left; some were further divided between upstairs and down, making space for four households altogether. The building style was old-fashioned, with the exterior covered in rough mortar, and small windows enclosed in sturdy wooden frames. Housing for doctors and other hospital employees, probably, but awfully dreary. Piles of junk, including twisted old bicycles and the crushed remains of a pen as small as a birdcage, once the home of some tiny animal, robbed the area of any sense of life. These houses looked more like special research laboratories of some sort, or even sickrooms. Or had the former residents all been evacuated to make room for some redevelopment project?

Finally the doctor stopped in front of one of the buildings. The path between structures was as crooked as a child's scrawl, and in addition the view was impeded by shrubbery, making conditions ideal for shadowing. By the same token, it was also extremely hard to judge relative positions. And this house had no particular distinguishing characteristics, except for a sign reading "E4" and a slightly greener tinge in its mortar. The man knew he could not have described how to get there from the tunnel, except to say it was a good ways back.

After watching the doctor check the mailbox and go upstairs, he ran through the garden, ducking under shrubbery, and peered inside. There were four mailboxes, but judging from the layers of dirt and rust, only one was now in use. The doctor's shadow was crouched over on the landing, facing away from a dirty transom window. He seemed to be having trouble with his key. It was the left-hand door on top, as you faced the building. The air was thick and amber-colored, and there was the smell of a dead animal. The man's body shook with an unpleasant foreboding. Suddenly his thoughts shrank like a piece of fat meat plunged into boiling water, then grew paper thin. This was not just some secret rendezvous; he sensed that his wife's very life was in danger. If this was still part of the hospital, they might even be conducting experiments on living creatures. Obscene experiments, so horrible that not even the nurses were allowed in.

Staying close to the wall, he went all around the house once. The back faced north-northeast. The window there was much smaller, probably for a kitchen or bathroom. When he came around front again after circling the house, over on the south side, which seemed to be divided into two rooms, all of a sudden a window toward the center slid open. Pressing flat against the wall, he listened with his whole body: a steamship's whistle, like a deep groaning wheeze; rumblings of the town, permeating every smallest corner; sounds of a helicopter flying somewhere. Nothing that resembled a human voice. Were the two of them on such intimate terms that they had no need to speak out loud, then, only whispering softly back and forth under their breath? Or was she gagged and bound, unable to converse at all? Perhaps the reason the doctor had appeared so calm at the spaghetti house was that she had already been made impervious to the effects of time.

He measured the distance to the window with his eyes, and groped around carefully for any protuberance that might serve as a foothold, any hollow that might provide a handgrip. Mentally he prepared to face a scene that he would far rather have avoided. The main thing now was revenge. He was already too deeply wounded to fear greater injury. Along the doorframe of the main entrance was a downspout. The location was not bad, but it was far too corroded to support his weight. At the same time, the window was too high to reach with his jump shoes. There had to be something he could do. On the building next door, directly above stairs leading to the flat roof, was a wedge-shaped structure that looked as though one side had been sliced off diagonally. That seemed to be the roof entrance. This building ought to have one, too, then. If an attack from below wouldn't work, he would try an attack from above.

He made his way softly up the stairs. There, just as he had expected, was another flight, continuing on up from the landing. The door at the top was padlocked, but the lock was so old and rusty that it fell apart with one twist, clasp and all. The hinges squeaked: a short, sharp sound like the squawk of a long-tailed rooster. He waited briefly, but there was no response. Luckily, no one seemed to have noticed. The sunlight was not too strong, but even so, its reflection off the rooftop hurt his eyes. A thick layer of baked dust crunched underfoot like crackers.

Getting down on his knees by a low, knee-high railing, he leaned out as far as he dared. The window awning was in the way, and all he could make out were the two ends of the frame on the open window. The metal awning was only fifteen centimeters wide at most; if he did make it down, it would be all he could do to gain a footing.

Suddenly from the room below came a moan. It was the voice of a woman. The sound was so depersonalized, however, that he was unable to say whether or not it was his wife. Then there was a short, muffled conversation, and again sporadic, low, stifled moans.

Taken by surprise, the man cowered, trembling, like a worm doused with boiling water. In his head was one thought only: to see inside that room. He hooked his shoetops around the base of the railing, held onto the downspout, and swung himself around. Hanging head down with his stomach against the wall, he realized glumly that it was now impossible to get back up. Luckily the downspout there was not as corroded as below. Anyway, he would try to lower himself down as far as he could. Then if the metal fixtures would just hold fast, he might be able to work his way around and burst in through the window. If his luck gave out and the downspout did break or collapse, he would give a good hard kick against the wall, do a backward somersault in the air, and then trust to the cushioning action of the jump shoes.

Short screams began to mix with the woman's moaning. He could make out a bed in one corner of the room. The doctor lay there naked, face up, on a white sheet. The blanket had fallen down on the floor, exposing the top of the bed to full view, but for some reason the woman was nowhere to be seen. Yet the voice went on as before. The source of the sound seemed to be a large speaker set up near the pillow. The entire wall was plastered with nude photographs, large and small. The voice from the speaker increased in sinuosity, filling the room with its intricate convolutions. Through it all the doctor lay applying some sort of instrument to the end of his erect penis, rotating his knees and vibrating his wrists at the rate of five times per second.

Their eyes met. The doctor sprang up, grabbing a towel near the pillow and wrapping it around his waist as he charged toward the window. Instinctively the man tightened his hold on the downspout. The doctor reached out an arm and grabbed the belt of his trousers. Trying to break free, the man jerked his hips, whereupon the downspout silently gave way. He hung momentarily in midair. The doctor tried to free himself, but unable to pull out his hand from under the belt, he fell headlong, dragged by the man's weight. Perhaps in trying to shield his erect penis, he had not braced himself as well as he should have.

The two men fell to the ground, still joined. On the way down they made a half-turn, so that when they landed the doctor was on the bottom. The man escaped with only a scrape or two, but the doctor had apparently hit his head; he lay there unconscious. His huge, white, hairy body lying face up on the ground stark naked, eyes wide open, was an eerie sight. He was still breathing, though, and his pulse was rapid but steady. Also, for better or for worse, his penis remained firmly erect.

The man was more perturbed by the doctor's erect penis than by his loss of consciousness. He covered the organ with the towel. It was still noticeable, but that was some improvement. His next impulse was to shut off that woman's voice, crying out in greater and greater agitation from above. At the same time he would be able to phone somewhere for help. A search would probably turn up a notebook with frequently dialed numbers in it. Anyway, he decided to go back up to the room. The door was locked from the inside. This time there was no need to worry about being seen, so he let himself down with both hands from the roof straight to the metal awning, swung around down, and jumped inside. He shut off the switch. The woman's last gasp stuck in the depths of his ears.

Before he could find the telephone, it began to ring of its own accord. There was no use hesitating. He let it ring three times and then picked up the receiver.

Immediately, a man's soothing voice came into his ear.

"It's all right, we understand the situation. Please just wait there a minute."

"Were you watching?"

"How is the injured person?"

"I think he's unconscious."

"Don't move him. If you can, cool his head with a damp cloth. And if there's an umbrella or something around, try to shield his face with it. We'll be right there."

It wasn't entirely the fault of that doddering old guard. Part of the responsibility was his for thinking that the guard's explanation had made sense, and falling for it hook, line, and sinker. He had got himself into a fine mess. Not only had it been a wild-goose chase as far as tracing his wife was concerned, but now he was in real hot water. For all he knew, he might even have to face the police. The voice over the phone had said it was all right, but what was all right? They understood the situation, he had said, but what situation? He didn't care for the implications. Maybe now was the time to make a getaway.

He decided to go back up to the roof to retrieve his briefcase and jacket. On his way out he had an idea; going back, he removed the tape of the woman's voice from the tape deck and stuck it in his back pocket. He left the door unlocked. A wind had come up. He walked around on the rooftop. The view there was more open than below on the ground, but less so than he had expected. Down in the south garden the doctor was still lying face up, penis erect as ever. Far off at sea, waves glittered like gold under torn, fleecy clouds. The tunnel leading to the little shopping street under the cliff would be in that direction. To the west, the housing area stretched as far as he could see. Instinctively he felt that the hospital buildings should be to the east, beyond the urban area, but a dense grove of maples cut off his view. Across to the north, the hills were joined directly to the sky; a single building in front was thrusting up its head. Only slightly lower than the red and white smokestacks of the incinerator plant on the left, it appeared to be fairly tall.

The sound of an engine began to come closer. Suddenly a white van was visible over the hills. Its motor seemed to be racing as it zoomed along among the dwellings, heading straight this way. Now was the time to escape. A few seconds' hesitation, however, and it was too late. Before he was all the way downstairs, the sound of squealing brakes blocked the front entrance. Now, rather than act suspiciously nervous, he would try to greet them calmly, and with good grace. He went back to the room.

Three men in white coats got out of the van, each wearing a slightly different type of uniform. No, two were men and one was a woman, her hair cut short in a boyish style. One of the men was thin and short, and the other was of medium height, with a barrel chest. All three looked up together at the room where he was. As though acting on behalf of the others, the fellow in the smallest white coat held up one finger, evidently a sign that they meant him no harm.

The small man bent over the prostrate doctor, peering at

his pupils and testing his reflexes with a quick, professional touch, while the other two looked on intently from a short distance. Gently he removed the towel and measured the length of the injured man's penis. He pinched and poked it, making notes. The woman averted her eyes and stood there awkwardly, scuffling her feet.

The stocky man brought out a stretcher from the back of the van. At that signal the woman started heading toward the house. The man was seized with panic. He felt as embarrassed as though his room were being invaded. Of course, she was tough enough to stand and watch a man's erect penis being measured, so perhaps she was no ordinary young woman.

"Hurry, come here."

She was in her late twenties, dark-skinned, with a hard, wiry build, and evidently strong-minded. Still, she was not as mannish as he had judged from her hair style, looking down from above.

He went out into the corridor to meet her, and began a lame explanation.

"It wasn't my fault. Everything—it's hard to explain, but . . ."

The woman nodded sympathetically, slipped past him, and entered the room. With a wry smile she surveyed the nude photographs on the wall, and headed straight for the bed. Gathering up several dozen sheets of tissue paper from the bedside, she lifted up the strange instrument with which the doctor had been masturbating.

"You know what this is?"

According to her, it was a receptacle for gathering sperm. The sperm bank had a purchasing system whereby price was computed on the basis of a donor's age, health status, physical strength, IQ, genetic factors, and so on, also taking into account aesthetic considerations. This particular doctor had been assessed at 1,280 yen per gram. The problem was that he had an ejaculation nearly every day. Even though not very many people were interested in artificial insemination, he kept making contributions, taking advantage of the purchasing system, until the bank's store of semen was so out of balance that if they weren't careful, a whole batch of babies looking like him might well be born. He seemed to have no particular zeal for progeny, however; he was only after the money. But even supposing he brought in a specimen every day for 365 days, after a year it would still come to less than 500,000 yen, so you could see what an old miser he was. That building, too, was going to be torn down before the year was out to make room for a bigger cemetery, and the water had already been shut off; he was only hanging on because the rent was free.

A voice from below called that it was time to leave.

The woman waved her arm from the window in response. "That short little man is the hospital's assistant director. He's in charge of cartilage surgery, too. I'm his secretary." As she identified herself, she searched in the emergency doctor's pants pockets and came up with a bunch of keys. Next she went to remove the tape from the cassette deck; finding it already gone, she turned and gave the man an arch look. He shifted his eyes, pretending not to see.

When they went downstairs, the emergency doctor had already been loaded into the back of the van, stretcher and all. The heavy-set man was in the driver's seat. The secretary seated herself beside him, so the man took a seat next to the assistant director, on a bench beside the stretcher.

The van began to move, and the air conditioning came on. Perhaps the interior of the ambulance that had carried away his wife had been like this. When they crossed over the ridge of hills, they came to a broad, paved street, beyond which a succession of two-story wooden row houses stretched parallel with a low, double-wired fence.

Clouds were rolling in from the west. It might rain.

"But why—"

Cutting off the man's words in midsentence, the assistant director lifted back the towel from the doctor's lower abdomen in front of him.

"How does that compare with yours? It's not exactly stunted, but for a man his size it isn't too impressive, is it? Of course, there isn't necessarily any direct connection between penis size and libido, but—"

"Where are we going?"

"We've got to get this man to the hospital right away."

"But I—"

"Why don't you wait in my office? As soon as I get him taken care of, I'll be right with you."

"I don't know what's going on."

"They say his spermatogenetic capacity is really something."

"I want to get to work so I can attend a conference this afternoon. . . ."

"You know, modern medicine understands next to nothing about the mechanism of erection."

The penis had begun to show small wrinkles, but when the assistant director flicked it with the tip of his finger, it swelled out again beautifully. Soon they passed beyond the rows of wooden buildings, and in front of them appeared the maple grove. Beyond an empty lot of red clay was a low-lying area that had been deeply dug out. From that valley, as though resting its elbow on the edge of the empty lot, rose a tall building. That would be the one he had seen from the top of E4. It had a good fifteen floors, narrowing in slightly at the top; on the bottom, giant arms spread out in all four directions like the legs of some monstrous bird that was menacingly clawing the ground.

The top of an arm was level with the red clay lot. They drove straight in, past pairs of white-coated men playing catch, into the center of the building. The man and the secretary were let off there, and the van drove away somewhere.

The assistant director's office was on the top floor.

(The forty-odd minutes after the white van drove off, while I was kept waiting in the assistant director's office, are completely missing from the tape. That's understandable: I spent most of the time stuffing down sandwiches and coffee that the secretary had ordered for me. My conversation with her was awkward and fragmented. Knowing she had seen through my secret about hiding the tape of the woman's voice in my back pocket, I felt uneasy about her very presence. Looking back now, I can't help thinking that she was aware of that, and included it in her calculations. At any rate, it was definitely not a time period that lent itself to recording. Next is the interview with the assistant director that I included in the beginning, and with that the first tape comes to an end.)

Now I am back in that room in E4, writing out these notes. This is the room covered with nude photographs, formerly occupied by the doctor who lost consciousness without losing his erection, inside the area earmarked for cemetery expansion. The assistant director let me have the key to it as a temporary place to sleep. The tape playback equipment is of fairly high quality, and except for the lack of running water, I have no complaints. The doctor is still unconscious, I understand, lying in a ward in the cartilage surgery department.

It is late at night. The time is nearly eleven o'clock. I have been working on these notes since early this morning, and finally managed to finish off the first cassette. But I've barely accomplished a third of what I set out to do. In terms of the number of days, it doesn't even amount to a sixth of it all. I hadn't imagined that writing was anywhere near this difficult.

I may have spent a little too much time on details. Picking out only the relevant sounds from tape segments packed with so much interfering noise that they are as dense as trampled felt, relying solely on memory, tends to become as intricate an operation as assembling a clock. If I were to organize everything perfectly and keep going, determined to stay up all night, I might be able to keep my promise by dawn. But I'm tired. The muscles in my right thumb ache from overuse. My writing has disintegrated. I think I'll quit here for tonight; whether I continue writing or not is something I'll think about again in the morning, after I have sounded out the horse once more about his intentions.

Frankly, I don't get it. I have the persistent feeling that the horse has put one over on me. No matter how precisely I may file my complaint, I'm afraid it will all come to nothing in the end. I suppose it will provide me with an alibi. But what I need right now isn't an alibi; I need some clues as to my wife's whereabouts. I have been provided with a white coat to enable me to walk around freely inside the hospital, and I've even been registered as a temporary employee. But all that could just be candy designed to divert my attention from other things and keep me pinned quietly to my desk here.

The horse has been awfully jumpy lately. With the hospital's founding anniversary only four days off, he seems to be in a hurry to put on the finishing touches. I can understand his desire to evade responsibility. Besides, he may have wanted to sound out my thinking in these notes. Nothing is so dangerous as betrayal by someone who knows too much. And from the horse's point of view, the fact that I am so healthy must be especially hard to take.

Drops of sweat running off the end of my nose have made three spots, lined up in a row on the page. I do think that this labor will help me somehow to preserve my sanity. On the edge of the black sea, where lights of squid-fishing boats appear and disappear, hangs a fat orange half-moon; somehow that familiar, banal sight fills me with horror tonight.

Already four days have passed since I stopped going to work. There is no going back now, I know.

Notebook Two

Notebook Two

At 4:43 a.m. I was startled from my sleep by a phone call from the horse.

In sharp contrast to my grouchiness from lack of sleep, the horse was in high spirits again this morning, no less than the day before. And true enough, his running was greatly improved, so like the real thing now it seemed a shame there was no accompanying noise of hoofbeats. The pacing and rhythm of his front and hind legs were precisely matched; each leg touched ground at a slightly different time, giving a smoothly integrated impression overall. Best of all was the way his body no longer bent and twisted. Without a sense of evenly interlocking motion, he tends to look like a play horse. My only complaint was his way of waving his arms to stabilize his upper body. That's an unfortunate habit; it almost makes him look as though he has six legs.

The horse cut short his practice and came bounding over toward me, flapping the bottom of his athletic shirt to let the air through. His face wore an expression of earnest questioning. I knew he was after my opinion of his performance, but I passed over it in silence. Handing him a sandwich and the thermos of coffee, I merely reported in a businesslike way that the notes were not yet completed.

To my surprise, the horse showed so much interest in that first unfinished notebook that he held on to it, saying he wanted to go over it again more carefully when he had time. He gave me money to buy a second notebook.

Without a moment's hesitation I served notice.

"I've had enough. All this playing hide-and-seek with myself isn't going to lead anywhere, no matter how long I keep it up. I feel no responsibility to carry out a deal when the conditions for payment are this vague."

With a look of calm bemusement, the horse glanced

thoughtfully through the last few pages before answering, rubbing his forehead with his fingertips.

"Seen through it, have you? Well, it could be you're right;
maybe these notebooks are a means of sounding out where you
stand, just as you suspect. But you seem to have the wrong idea
about the purpose of it all. Any question about your loyalties is
centered on your attitude toward your wife. How serious are
you about looking for her? That's what I've got to make sure
of. . . ."

"There you go again. That's just what I don't like." I
wasn't yielding any ground. "A man's wife doesn't go around
getting lost every day, you know, so if she disappears, of course
I'm going to look for her. You keep switching the point; that's
why I can't trust you any more."

"Don't go too far, now." He shifted his weight to his back
legs and crossed his front legs in a rather unhorsy way. Then,
pouring himself a second cup of coffee, he went on: "I'm already doing everything I can to help you."

"Like what?"

"Like—come on; I gave you the key to solving the riddle
of how your wife managed to disappear from that sealed-box
waiting room, didn't I?"

"When was that?"

"Don't tell me you didn't even notice!"

"Come off it, will you?"

"The very beginning of the tape, right after it starts to
play."

"Oh, if that's what you mean, I couldn't figure that part
out. It's all in the notebook, but in the first place, at that point
nobody could possibly have known yet who I was or what I'd
come for. . . ."

"Are you talking about your conversation in the street
with the lady from the Mano Agency?"

"No matter how I figure it, it seems awfully strange that
you were keeping tabs on me that soon. It completely con-
tradicts what security told me about the bugs they planted,
and . . ."

"That was different. It wasn't aimed at you in particular.

All conversations with service agency customers are monitored in the general diagnostic room, on principle. In order to assemble all the data on you, we put in a special request to the recording supervisor there and got a copy of their tape. Just try comparing it with the parts that security did; the sound quality is completely different. You know, I think it's high time you understood how the hospital really works. Improving the medical care system and streamlining the administration are two goals that aren't always compatible. It's certainly not desirable to have to use the agencies as we do, but as things stand it's a necessary evil."

As a recent example, the horse told me about one unfortunate patient. A certain middle-aged man was waiting for a bus, when a girl rode past the bus stop on a bicycle, riding one-handed and carrying a transparent plastic bag filled with about fifty eggs. She seemed to be a beginner on the bike, and handled the bars unsteadily. Just then two trucks approached from opposite directions. As they passed each other, they would occupy between them the entire width of the road. From where the man stood, it looked as though they would come together right next to the girl on the bicycle. In his imagination her bike crashed into a telephone pole and the plastic bag was knocked against a cement wall. The next instant, when the fifty eggs smashed into one slimy yellow mass, rose vividly in his mind's eye. He felt sick, doubled over, and passed out. (For the record, the trucks passed safely without harm to the girl, and the plastic bag contained Ping-pong balls.)

In thirteen minutes an ambulance arrived. Since it was daytime, an agency representative took care of the business details of hospital admittance. The agent's questioning was relayed by walkie-talkie to the general diagnostic room, where it was attended by six specialists stationed in front of speakers, waiting for patients. Their specialties were peripheral circulatory organs, endocrinology, cell metabolism, neurosurgery, medicinal poisoning, and sensory nerves, all relatively small fields.

Agents are bound by agreement to persuade the patients to comply with the opinion of the diagnostic room. However, as a rule, when the wishes of the patient or his family are known they must be honored. As a result, most cases tend to gravitate to the general departments of internal medicine, surgery, and psychiatry. The patient cannot very well be blamed for not properly understanding the nature of his own illness, but the situation poses a grave problem for the minor departments. There are even extreme cases, it seems, in which the entire caseload of a department consists of doctors and nurses from the hospital who register as patients out of a sense of duty. Ideally, it would be best to lump all the general departments together into one diagnostic department, but administratively it makes much more sense just to get rid of all the specialists who are so hard up for patients. Every year the scramble for patients becomes more and more intense as departments try desperately to improve their records in order to stave off budget cuts.

The middle-aged man, since he was still unconscious and unaccompanied by any family members, represented an unparalleled boon to the crowd of specialists. Besides, according to eyewitnesses—none of whom would have dreamed of blaming a girl carrying eggs on a bicycle—it was a case of utterly unprovoked fainting. The patient was not very advanced in years, showed no signs of infirmity, had experienced no convulsions or spasms, and yet was still unconscious. It was hardly surprising that every department claimed him for its own. Ordinarily the specialists would come to an agreement after a certain amount of consultation, but on this occasion tempers flared, and each man stubbornly pressed his own case without yielding. Finally it turned into an ugly mud-slinging contest, with allegations being hurled right and left about this one's philandering and that one's game of chess.

The agent, meanwhile, could not complete his papers without an answer from the diagnostic center; while he fretted away the time, the patient's condition took a sudden turn for the worse, resulting in death. And so the doctors' prize was finally snatched from them by the resuscitation department.

In the resuscitation department, the middle-aged man started to breathe again. Since that department takes little interest in treating illnesses, however, they merely accepted his thanks and released him right away, shortly after which he died again. But the resuscitation department lives fully up to its name; even now, at intervals of every four or five days he dies and comes back to life, then dies and comes back to life again, his waking hours one long hymn of gratitude.

"What's all that got to do with my wife?"

"I never said it had anything to do with her."

"You did, too. You said the key to the riddle of the sealed room, or something, was on the beginning of the tape."

"That comes even earlier. It's only about ten seconds or so, very short, but it's there."

"It is not."

"You missed it, then. You must have thought it was just noise, and skipped over it. When you get back, listen to it carefully again."

"What is there to hear?"

"After you've listened to it, why don't we go into that subject together?"

"If there's that obvious a clue lying around, then shouldn't we do something about it right now, not sit around wasting time on these damn notebooks? . . ."

"You're the one who's wasting time. Or have you got some reason why you don't want to move ahead with it, and is that why you've purposely put on the brakes?"

"You're too suspicious."

"I hope so. But tell me, if a ship vanished without a trace, leaving only an SOS, would you just send out a rescue boat? Why not try a lighthouse, too? Action is all very well, but shouldn't you do more than just sniff around like a dog? It seems to me that lighting up the way back is a perfectly good, realistic step to take. My real intention with these notebooks is to use them as a sort of map to guide your wife back with. See? Wait until the results are in before you decide if this is such a thankless job or not."

I didn't see, but I'd been outmaneuvered. Feeling sour, unable to argue back, I thought I understood why innocent people confess to crimes they never did. Leaving the horse, I went back to my room and immediately started playing back the first tape. Sure enough, when I listened carefully there were indeed some very suggestive sounds.

I went out to the basement of the main building to buy a second notebook. While there I rode the elevator up to the top floor and poked my head inside the assistant director's office. The secretary had just come to work. Picking up two pep pills and a key, I went across the hall to the security room. I wanted to have a look at the floor plan for mikes around the outpatient waiting room. There was only one, it turned out, inside the pharmacy. I figured that knowing the position of the micro-phone might make it easier to analyze the sounds on the tape. I must have been a little excited. Shaking off the secretary, who was full of questions about the horse and seemed to have other things she wanted to talk about, too, I hurried back to my room.

First I made a rough floor plan of the outpatient waiting room, including the pharmacy. I marked out the position of the mike. Then, mentally stationing myself there, I listened to the start of the tape over and over, tracing changes in tone and volume over the twin axes of time and space, reconstructing them. What was at first mere noise gradually took shape as a distinct scene.

The sound of wind rattling window panes in the pharmacy . . . wait, the wind hadn't come up till well after sunrise . . . maybe it was the air conditioner . . . footsteps coming closer . . . rubber-soled sandals . . . coming closer, hesitating, suddenly distinct . . . no, that wasn't it, it was just that the background noise had suddenly stopped . . . the footsteps kept coming closer, still hesitating . . . what kind of natural sound would stop so sud-denly? Let's hear it once more . . . maybe I was stretching things, but it sounded to my imagination as if someone were fooling around with the pharmacy shelves . . . the footsteps stopped . . . a momentary pause, then a sharp, metallic sound . . . then, from somewhere nearby, a dull, heavy thud. . . .

.   .   .

And so I have continued writing. There doesn't seem to be any choice but to go along with this deal. The horse definitely knows something. The very fact that he put those noises at the beginning of the tapes proves he has more information than I do—and it could be more than just information.

What bothers me is how he plans to use these reports. What was his real meaning in calling them a map to help my wife out of the labyrinth? I hope he isn't going to blame whatever happens on the results of this investigation. The next time I give him one of these notebooks, I'm going to attach some conditions. In exchange for my promise not to pull any tricks on him, I want a clear account of what they're being used for, and a guarantee of my right to strike out any parts that I might consider self-damaging.

(The second tape begins with my introduction to the chief of security by the secretary, after meeting with the assistant director. The security room is on the same floor, just across the hall. As we crossed the hallway the secretary whispered to me, "The assistant director is impotent." Even the widest corridor takes only a few moments to cross. I had no time to think of an answer—but it's about time that "I" went back to the third person. The man had no idea how to reply. She didn't seem out to smear the assistant director in particular, so perhaps rather than elicit a specific response, she wanted only to make a strong impression. In that case she succeeded. As soon as a woman brings up any matter relating to sex, a man egotistically assumes that she is being deliberately provocative. Besides, it was only a short time after he and she had shared the unusual experience of viewing the emergency doctor's erection at close range, in broad daylight, and so very likely a certain sense of camaraderie was at play.)

The security room was a near-match for the assistant director's office in both size and shape. Just inside was another door that led to an adjoining room, corresponding to the secretary's office.

The broad, double-paned window at the far end of the room ensured both light and quiet. Even the set of chairs, black synthetic leather over metal pipes, was exactly the same. There the similarities ended, however. The assistant director's office was decorated with great simplicity; apart from some touches of color in the frame of a sketch of two mating horses, everything else, from the carpet to the plastic calendar, was the same, or nearly the same, shade of blue-gray as the walls. In comparison, this room was a riot of confusion. Every wall in sight was covered with panels of dials and switches, with bunches of multicolored electrical wires weaving between them, stretching every which way and hanging down to the floor, which was stacked with tools and parts. With a little more organization or coherence, it might have resembled a broadcasting studio or a computer room, but without any sense of planning it was more like a wholesale supply house for spare electrical parts.

A man in white, hunched over a workbench by the window, his back to the door, swung around in his revolving chair and removed his headphones.

"Hello again there. I should have mentioned this before, but I'm the chief of security."

It was the driver of the white van, who had driven off with the assistant director before. The man was partly relieved to have met him already, and partly suspicious. Every last little thing seemed just too coincidental. . . .

The chief went on talking, as though he had seen through the man's distrust. He spoke rapidly, in a carefully controlled voice that somehow called attention to his throat muscles.

"No, don't bother to introduce yourself. No need for any introductory remarks, either. I know all about you."

"But how . . ."

The chief raised a fat, fleshy palm and silenced him. Picking up a black instrument about five centimeters square from the workbench, he flicked a switch. A thin noise like the whining of a mosquito started up. Smiling in a satisfied way, lower lip thrust out, he half rose, extending the implement across the table toward the man. The mosquito became a horsefly. At the man's left coat pocket, the noise turned into a harsh electrical buzz.

"Let's have a look at what's in there."

"This . . ."

"I know; it's a woman's rented garment, right?"

There was no help for it if he knew already. Reluctantly the man pulled out the wad of beige cloth that had been stuffed to bursting in his pocket. The chief removed the belt of the dress with a practiced hand, opened the back of the buckle with a fingernail, and plucked out a pair of small mercury batteries. The noise of the instrument ceased immediately.

"You're kidding me."

"It's an FM transmitter. Since you were carrying this around the whole time, it was child's play to follow everything you did. Once you see how it works there's no mystery to it, eh? Now you know how we were able to make it to the scene of the accident before, just in the nick of time."

"That's a pretty rotten trick. Now that you mention it, that old guy at the agency said he used to be a magician. . . ."

"That's got nothing to do with it. It isn't only that one store. There's a tiny transmitter inside every rented costume and accessory."

The chief struck his heel lightly against the floor, spinning his chair around, then leaned forward and began manipulating a big panel left of the workbench. The wall beside it was crammed full of tape decks, nine rows down and six across, making fifty-four in all, their reels all facing outward. Several of the reels were slowly turning; now and then one would stop and another would start, but there seemed to be no special sequence.

From a corner of the room came the mutter of voices. They were from a speaker, but the fact that they were hidden made the sound incredibly lifelike, as though the owners of the voices were there in the room. They were not discussing much of anything; it was a man and woman counting up money, but the sound was so graphically real that somehow it seemed wrong to listen in. Speakers and amps probably had something to do with it, but that was not all. It was their way of abbreviating everything they said in such a way that it was comprehensible to the two of them, but to no one else.

"This is take-out B3 . . . doesn't seem to be very interesting, does it."

The chief turned off the switch and explained. Except for a few special cases, renting clothes from one of the agencies nearly always meant a "take-out"—the man himself had been mistaken for one. A "take-out" simply meant escorting a patient out of the ward or area where he or she was supposed to be.

Most of the hospital inpatients, however, had no street clothes. They were allowed to see visitors in their own rooms or in the interview rooms, and any who were considered well enough to go outside were outpatients anyway. It was one thing for single patients to hide street clothes, but when married patients did it they invited the suspicion of the spouses, which frequently led to a family quarrel.

What kind of people would go to all the trouble of bringing in rented clothes to patients? The answer was simple: adulterers. Perhaps because their lack of street clothes furnished a handy alibi, patients would become quite bold sexually. For both men and women, the rate of illicit intercourse among hospital patients was said to be something like 3.5 to four times that among ordinary people. There was even a special clothing-delivery service for secret rendezvous between patients. (On this point I should mention that the assistant director did not agree that the sexual desires of patients were directly attributable to their mere possession or lack of streetwear. I will touch on this again in more detail later as part of the assistant director's philosophy of patients, but for now I will simply point out that his view differed.)

Once the problem of clothing was solved, next came finding a suitable place. For those whose sexual needs could be taken care of with a simple back scratch or so, place was no particular problem. Inside the maple grove that covered the entire southeastern slope surrounding the main building and the red clay lot was a cemetery owned and operated by the hospital. The gravestones were flat, the trees provided abundant shade, and even the farthest ward was within a ten-minute walk. The difficulty was that there were too many centipedes; besides, tetanus bacilli had been detected in the soil, so it was necessary to be on guard against any violent activity that might involve the danger of external injury. In such a case there was likely to be a sense of constraint in such open surroundings anyway, making it preferable to remain indoors after all. Fortunately, inside the urban area that encroached on the valley between the main building and the outpatient wing were a dozen or more love hotels aimed at such clientele, mouths pursed up like tiny holes, open and waiting.

The security room window afforded a fine lookout over their relative positions. Into a hollow between two elevations in the ground, shaped like the curved neck of a gourd, ran the two-lane trunk highway out of the northwest. Passing through a tunnel under the saddle between the hills, it headed off toward the sea. Both sides of the highway were densely packed with stores, offices, and apartment buildings; the boundary between that urban area and the hospital area, however, was not clear-cut. The main hospital building was of simple construction, with the tall, narrow central section supported firmly by four rectangular blocks at the base. The outpatient wing, however, was nothing but a cluster of structures piled up haphazardly on the hill, looking somewhat like an old battleship.

The man was able to gain some idea of the route he must have taken in shadowing the emergency doctor. First they had gone along the inner side of the main building, following the boundary line with the urban area until just before the highway. Then, taking the underpass and coming out by the sea, they had come back through the Jizō tunnel and finally arrived on the other side of the hill. Unfortunately, that lay in a blind spot from the security room window; presumably, it was in the direction of the Himalayan cedar, bent over with the weight of its branches, that completely hides the left front of this room where I am now writing in this notebook. According to the security chief, these uninhabited houses in the projected cemetery expansion site are quite popular with people who use them. As long as you didn't mind going without amenities like a shower before and after, or use of a toilet, they probably would make pretty good secret meeting places, at that.

The chief and the acting director were strongly interested in the sexual impulses of these adulterers, and decided to try eavesdropping on them. By sheer chance they had such unexpectedly good results the first time that it became a passion with them both. However, there was no way of guaranteeing that their prey would always oblige them by going as hoped to a place that had previously been bugged. At the same time it was too impractical to try to bug each and every place that could conceivably be used for a rendezvous. Complications with monitors, the expense of maintaining batteries, the trouble of changing them (in continual use they last about eighty hours) . . . too much waste was involved. After repeated trial and error, they finally hit upon the plan of enlisting the service agencies to insert small FM transmitters inside rented clothing, which was essential for a take-out. As a result, they were now able to get a bead on all the heavy romances, effectively and securely.

"I don't know what the point of all this is, but it's too damned kinky for me."

"Go ahead and talk; that little item you sneaked out of the emergency doctor's room is still there inside your pants pocket, isn't it?"

Cornered, the man went on the defensive. Just how serious was the chief about helping him search for his wife? To convey his irritation he glanced openly at his wrist watch several times, but the chief paid not the slightest attention. Indicating the fifty-four tape recorders behind him with a thumb over one shoulder, he went on complacently.

Already an organization had been formed, made up of over four thousand fans of these rendezvous tapes. For a monthly fee of two thousand yen it was possible to rent out a new one every month. Proceeds came to nearly one hundred million yen a year. For the security room that was an important source of revenue, thanks to which they had been able to purchase three high-speed transcribers. At the end of last year they had introduced a microcomputer, so that automatic recording of love scenes was now possible. Whenever a take-out customer appeared, the agency involved would phone the security room and report the code number of the transmitter out on loan. When that number was fed into the computer, the sound-oscillating repeater would go to work, picking up the sound of clothing being removed, and the deck in the security room would automatically begin recording. At present, they could handle up to eight thousand subscribers with no difficulty.

"But your case, now, was a little different." The chief dropped his voice and stared down at the thick acrylic resin table. His eyes, reflected there upside down, stared back up inquisitively at the man. "Because usually take-outs don't start until around two p.m. at the earliest. And there you were right off the bat, first thing in the morning. Somehow I didn't feel like leaving it up to automatic recording, so I listened in from the start. But it was all for the best, wasn't it, since as it turned out we made it there before it was too late. . . ."

At last they seemed to be coming back to the mainstream. The man held carefully to the rudder, trying not to steer off course.

"I don't know about that. Maybe it's already too late, as far as I'm concerned."

"Don't be so fainthearted; that's a no-no." When he smiled his mouth became almost circular, the canine teeth like placid retrograde animals. "The emergency doctor's condition still isn't too good, but for the time being nobody's planning any action against you on suspicion of accidental infliction of injury, or illegal entry."

Casually, but unerringly, he drove the nail home. The man was not about to be taken in by any round-mouthed grin.

"It was out of my control. I didn't know what was going on, and then that guard, the one and only witness, went and told me a story so plausible and believable . . ."

He pulled out the day's sixth cigarette and put it in his mouth.

"No smoking." The chief gave the reprimand tonelessly. "You don't need to worry about that guard, either. We've taken care of him. He may have sent a deposition to the assistant director; shall I find out?"

He pressed a button on the interphone and called the station.

The station, on the ground floor of the same building, was for the security force. At any given time of day or night, eighteen security personnel were on duty, defending their posts in eight-hour shifts. What with delivering rendezvous tapes to subscribers, collecting fees, soliciting and enrolling new members, patrolling specified areas, and going out on emergency calls involving quarrels or burglaries, there was plenty of work to keep them all busy. In particular, replacing worn-out batteries for all the two hundred and some dozen fixed bugs was a big job; strong-legged young men would go around together in pairs (since much of the work could only be done riding on someone else's shoulders) and get the job done in half the time it would take one person. That time when the man had been taking a leak out by the alley near the spaghetti house while waiting for the doctor, the shaven-headed duo in sweat pants who had suddenly appeared and jabbed him in the side had been such a pair. They had meant no harm, it seemed, but had merely gone by to check up on him, following walkie-talkie instructions from the chief.

All the men on outside duty, including those two, were patients from the ear and nose, dermatology, or psychiatric wards; a lot of them were into karate and judo, so if he handled it right he should have a lot of customers for his jump shoes, the chief added, skillfully employing just the right words to stir up the man's fighting spirit.

The buzzer on the interphone sounded, and someone who slurred his words like a student reported back. When they sent the guard somewhere or other, they had sent his deposition along with him. The chief explained that the somewhere or other, the name of which the man had been unable to catch, was the Psycholinguistics Center; to back up the guard's testimony, they had taken him there for a lie detector test.

The chief called the Psycholinguistics Center to see about the test results. The detailed analysis was not yet in, but so far it appeared that in the main the guard was telling the truth.

"That was the assistant director's wife." The chief put

down the receiver and spoke as if he had a condom on his tongue. "They're separated now, but she's quite an authority on lie detectors."

"Any new facts turn up in his testimony?"

"Not likely." He peered inside the back of the buckle on that rented dress. "Your code number is M-73F, so you might as well remember it. With that code number it's possible to isolate all the segments having to do with you from all these tapes, at any time. Your information is pretty accurate, though, isn't it?"

"Are you kidding? All I've heard yet is this insane story that she's vanished from someplace that it's impossible to escape from. I guess the information that there is no information is one kind of information, all right, but . . ."

The telephone rang. It was a notice of the second (or, not counting the man, the first) take-out customer of the day. She was a tall, dark woman of thirty-two or -three, and the clothes she had rented were a loud T-shirt and narrow bell bottoms, the sort of thing that would appeal to a young man. As he operated the computer's input unit, the chief murmured in a muffled, rather breathy voice, "There's a big difference between seeing and hearing. A lot of people find this system rather disappointing."

Seated on his chair, the man moved his center of gravity forward. He felt like a cat teased once too often that had instinctively ruffled its fur.

"So, getting right down to brass tacks—can I get some kind of assistance from you or not?"

"I suppose there isn't any choice; not with the direct recommendation of the assistant director behind you." The chief lifted his chin and slowly stroked the back of his hand up over his fat throat. "As you see, normally I'm the only one here in this room. I don't even let the other security personnel in here very often. The impact of this information is too great. You're the first person from the outside that I've ever let in."

"But if I don't find some new clues, I'm stuck in the same old dead end."

"It depends on you, and how hard you're willing to try."

"The assistant director said I should sound out the cleaning women, but . . ."

"That's a waste of time. When you read the guard's deposition, you'll see what happened during the transfer to the day shift. He didn't unlock the custodians' passageway until he had checked again and again to be absolutely sure that nobody was there. There were positively no witnesses."

"Then what am I supposed to do?"

The man's voice was shrill; the fingers of both hands were tightly clutching the chair arms. The chief gave a childish grin with that cylindrical mouth, and the superfluous flesh on his face puffed out under his eyes like a pair of buns.

"Don't worry, I'm going to let you use the playback room next door for a while. That ought to satisfy you. You can become dozens of invisible men simultaneously, walking around and sniffing out the whole hospital." The chief reached down and brought out a freshly laundered and starched white coat from a shelf beneath the workbench. With a deft twist of a knife he reduced the three black stripes on its breast pocket to one. "For now, until your position is officially settled, I'll let you use this. It's handy for getting in and out of the dining hall."

The starchy material filled the room with a pleasant, dry crackle. It was too wide in the shoulders, but the length was perfect. Calling to the man to follow, the chief crawled through a gap in the machinery, opened a door in the wall, and beckoned him into the adjoining room.

(With the sound of that door closing, the first side of tape two comes to an end, leaving an empty space of a dozen seconds or so. Actually, nearly five hours went by in that dozen seconds. Not that what happened then wasn't important. From the man's point of view, it was an extremely satisfying period of time. Finally, nine hours after his wife had disappeared, he was able to begin the genuine investigation. In that small cubbyhole, just as the chief had said, he was able to divide himself into dozens of selves at once as if with a magic mirror, appearing and disappearing at will from every corner of the grounds without ever moving, sticking in his nose and looking around as he pleased.)

At first he felt an almost painful sense of oppression, and faltered. It was as though he had jumped into midair with a parachute. Of course, he had never done such a thing in real life. Skydiving, it was called. You didn't open your parachute right away, but let the wind pressure distort your face as you clung belly-down like a bug to a log that wasn't there, falling straight down toward far-off ground that looked like an aerial photograph. It wasn't so much a fall as a loss of the external world. Perhaps the reason that he could understand the sensation without ever having experienced it was that it resembled a certain kind of awakening.

The sound of a beer bottle rolling across a tiled floor . . . the voice of a middle-aged woman, angry that the air conditioning is turned too high . . . someone's frightened breathing, age uncertain, and the businesslike, slightly irritated voice of a man, offering encouragement in trite phrases . . . slippers running hurriedly by . . . curses of someone bombarded with damp laundry . . . "Okay? Look, I mean, you know . . ." "Well, in general, I guess." "Shall we resign ourselves, then, or what?" "Well, hmm, that's about the size of it" . . . the sound of urinating, or perhaps of water being poured into a cup from a faucet . . . aluminum cans rolling and falling downstairs . . . sounds of a woman's panting; suppressed laughter; paper being torn . . . off-key whistling, like wind through a crack . . . kittens mewing . . . "Now, how shall I put it, uh, you know?" . . .

Since it was a special one-track (all one direction), six-channel recording system, a total of six unrelated sound sequences could be heard simultaneously, three from each headphone. He had to divide his attention among all six at the same time. Some of the sounds went on for a fairly long time, while others lasted only two or three seconds. Some scenes came and went again and again, tenaciously, while others flashed by momentarily, never to reappear. The selection was controlled by microcomputer. First the relayer would begin to work in response to sudden changes in tone or volume; it was programmed to stop recording automatically when the vocal-tension index fell below 3.2 in the case of human voices, or, in the case of other natural sounds, when rhythm and pitch were repeated in fixed patterns. The vocal-tension index was the quantification of physical response to psychological tension, he learned, while the repetition rate of natural sounds was understood to be the reverse function of background activities.

Therefore, even with channels of limited capacity it was possible to handle vast numbers of sound sources. In the past year, the total number of relayers had reached 214; each one had a receiving area of approximately one hundred meters radius, with a capacity of eight channels, so that a total of 1,712 circuits could be in simultaneous use. The entire hospital, virtually without exception, was thus under constant surveillance.

The man listened intently to those six interwoven time bands, their flow interrupted by jumps and skips, carefully sifting through the sounds in search of the slightest fragment that might be his wife's voice. Whenever a certain voice attracted him he could stop the tape and by manipulating switches on the control board play it back again and again as many times as he liked, until he was satisfied. Also, by decoding the pulse engraved on the head of that section of tape, he could find out the number of the relayer from which it had come, and even estimate the location of the concealed microphone with considerable accuracy.

He concentrated all his powers of attention on listening. Out of consideration for the long hours of work ahead, perhaps, a double curtain of black gauze covered the window, and a one-armed sofa with soft cushions had even been provided. If it turned out that he did find his wife this way, though, wouldn't it be a little too good to be true? He could not rid himself of a rather forlorn feeling, as though he were trying to scoop up water fleas with a basketball net. No matter how serious a matter this was to him, to the hospital it was doubtless simply the small misfortune of one outsider. If this intensive surveillance system did indeed have all the power that the chief had indicated, then his generosity in so casually yielding up his sanctum was all the more puzzling. The man was not so vain as to imagine that he was worth bothering to deceive, and yet the more he thought, the surer he became that he was being taken in. He couldn't help thinking that the proper course of action would have been to pour more energy into the less glamorous job of snooping around on foot.

Without the least regard for such misgivings, however, sounds came pouring out incessantly one after another, toying mercilessly with his emotions. Faint hope for the next instant diverted him each time from his doubts, keeping him pinned where he sat. Every sound, every voice, seemed to flash a clue in front of him. He could not be sure whether he only imagined it, starving for leads as he was, or whether there actually was some cryptogram hidden within the mass of sounds. In any case, it was an incredible barrage. Servility, anger, displeasure, excuses, scornful laughter, insinuations, jealousy, curses . . . and, permeating each and all of these, a slight indecency. The whispers, especially, were just like the rear view of a human being straddling a toilet bowl. When guilty shame wears a mask of curiosity, men are turned inside out, becoming strangers to themselves. Acute eavesdropping toxemia. The crumbling of his relationship to the outer world, based formerly on his sense of sight, brought on a dizziness like that caused by fear of heights. A time mosaic: moments that existed simultaneously, yet were impossible to experience simultaneously. It was like utter darkness.

The sense of hearing, compared to the sense of sight, is a fairly passive thing. It is possible to eradicate even a fifty-ton mammoth tanker just by closing the eyes, but it is almost impossible to escape the whirring wings of a single mosquito. By the same token, a barnacle on a tanker's hull is easily distinguishable, whereas great effort is required to pick out one particular set of footsteps from a noisy throng in the street. The rate of fatigue is likewise that much greater.

He was beginning to reach his limits. His neck muscles were as swollen as if he were wearing a lead hat, and the front of his head had started to throb, packed full of his distended eyeballs pressing out of their sockets.

Then suddenly it hit him. Maybe his wife had long since gone back home, and was there waiting for him even now. Yes . . . yes, of course . . . by now she would be worrying about where he was, phoning everywhere in search of him. He looked at his watch and discovered that it was already after six. That meant nearly five hours spent huddled over the control board. He had notified the office that he would be late to work, and then never called back. He would be hard put now to make amends for absenting himself without leave from the important conference that the company president had been scheduled to attend.

For the present, however, he had to relieve the pressure on his bladder, which was intolerable. Without bothering to notify the security room next door, he stepped outside through another door leading directly to the corridor and ran, scuffling his feet along the quiet ocher porcelain tiles, to the lavatory beside the elevator.

(The tape begins again here. This is the back of the second cassette. This time, however, since the microphone was not traveling around with me any longer as the FM transmitter in the belt of that rented dress had done, the sound quality and volume are uneven. Moving footsteps . . . noise of urinating . . . then a door opening and closing . . . an overall effect of ragged pieces of time joined together piecemeal. . . .

The phone rang. It was the horse, asking about my progress with these notes. I parried with a question of my own. Just as he had said, recorded on the very beginning of the first cassette were the sound of footsteps, and a vaguely suggestive atmosphere; he had to have some basis for calling that a lead. I

wanted his frank opinion, right away. If he withheld information from me, that was only going to deepen our mutual distrust.

The horse responded by inviting me to share a late supper
with him. He said he preferred to give me a detailed explanation then. In return, he attached the condition that I finish up at
least the second tape. I have a general idea of what it is he's
after. All right, so be it. The horizon out my window has disappeared, sea merging imperceptibly into sky. It looks as if it will
start raining in earnest.

I decided to take a break. I lit my eighth cigarette, poured
hot water from a thermos into a plastic cup of instant noodles,
and sipped on a can of Coke while I waited until it was ready to
eat. I took out my contact lenses and gave myself some eye
drops.)

When he came back from the lavatory, the door from the assistant director's office was standing ajar, as though waiting for
him. The secretary was peering through the crack in the door,
smiling, her face half hidden. He couldn't go by without saying
something.

"Okay if I use the phone?"

She nudged the door open with her hip and quickly disappeared inside. Was she inviting him in? Or was she trying to
speak as little as possible, on guard against some hidden microphone?

"Close the door." She spoke in a whisper and perched
herself on the arm of a sofa by the wall. "Dial zero for outside
calls."

"It'll only take a minute."

The phone was a new improved model, and the dial spun
around lightly. Listening to the first ring, he mentally reviewed
all the bizarre events of that day, feeling as though he had
finally reached shelter from a rainstorm. Why hadn't he thought
of this sooner? In a few seconds, at the other end of the line his
wife would pick up the receiver; in the next moment the curtains would part and sunlight pour through, and all the phan-

toms on the screen would vanish away. He would run straight out and be damned if he ever had anything to do with this place again. He could sense his own health starting to shine glossily under his skin, like blue neon.

The bell kept ringing.

"No answer, huh?"

"I'm calling home."

As the secretary shifted her position on the armrest, the front of her white coat parted, exposing one leg all the way to the top of the thigh. Her sleek, sunburned skin was as smooth as wax. Didn't she have anything on under her white coat except underwear, then?

The number of rings passed ten.

"Looks like nobody's home."

"She's probably busy and can't get away, out in the kitchen frying dinner or something. . . ."

The secretary did not reply. Without attempting to fix the hem of her uniform, although she must have been aware of his stare, she tapped out a light rhythm with her bare toes, legs stretched out. He felt a sudden urge to put his fingers in the dimples in her kneecaps.

The phone kept ringing. At the thirty-fifth ring he quit trying. The secretary stood up. Closing the front of her uniform, she covered her knees. Sometimes when a self-centered woman is being deliberately flirtatious she behaves with that sort of unpredictability.

"The employees' dining hall closes at eight-thirty. If you want, why don't you come with me?"

"I have one other call to make."

Peering at his hand as he spun the dial, the secretary rested her chin on the man's shoulder as she spoke.

"Your office."

"How did you know?"

"But nobody'll be there now."

A recorded voice answered.

Today's business hours ended at six o'clock. Thank you.

As he replaced the receiver, there was a far-off sound like the tinkle of a bell on a Buddhist altar. It was like waking from a dream of falling, only to find that he was still falling in real life.

"That coat doesn't fit you too well, but as long as it's right inside the building . . ." Looking up at him, she pulled on the button of her own collar. Her low-cut brassiere was purplish-red, a color that only goes well with light skin. "I have a meal ticket for you from the assistant director, but you'll have to pay for any drinks on your own, okay?"

"I don't feel like eating yet."

"You've got a lot of work ahead of you, though, don't you?"

Urging him to come along, she preceded him out into the corridor. The man followed behind, but then planted his feet down firmly to signify he meant to go no farther.

"I've got to hurry and do the rest of those tapes. . . ."

"But you've barely finished the first reel! There's no point in being in such a hurry."

"Are there a lot more?"

He felt as though he had licked the blade of a safety razor. The secretary opened her mouth so wide he could have peered down her throat, and laughed noiselessly.

"Of course! There are hundreds, thousands of hidden microphones all over the hospital. How could they all fit on just six channels?" She cut back across the corridor diagonally, opened the security room door without knocking, and poked her head inside. "How many reels so far today?"

The chief's resonant voice came booming back, as if he had been waiting to be asked.

"Six and a half."

"Just this morning?"

"That's right, up till noon. . . ."

Closing the door with an elbow, she spun around on one heel and came back, the rubber soles of her red sandals making short little squeaks. As she brushed by, she wound her arm around his, but the man broke away, his mind elsewhere.

"I've been tricked."

"What do you mean? . . ."

"It takes seven hours to listen to one hour's worth, then.

It's like playing hide-and-seek with my own shadow while it stretches out longer and longer. I'll never be able to catch up."

"But you're the only one who could pick out your wife's voice. You can't expect anybody else to help."

"This is like trying to catch the bullet train on a bicycle."

"Isn't that what reality is like? In a lottery, nothing says first prize can't turn up until all the lots are drawn."

Perhaps she was right. He could see that days spent in prison counting until the end of one's term would be far more real than a dream of innocence in a detention center. But if this was reality, then what of those peaceful days before his wife was carried off; were they only a memory? All at once it seemed the tender hairs on his wife's ear lobe brushed against the tip of his nose, like a soft wisp of air.

This time the secretary wrapped her eyes around him instead of her arm. She was a woman whose outlines were disturbingly distinct. His impression of his wife, by contrast, was as pale and light as beaten egg whites.

"Cheer up; stop looking as if you'd watched too many late late shows on TV. . . ."

Running her eyes swiftly along the line between ceiling and wall, she put a finger to her lips and quickly began walking. Dragged along by the dramatic gesture, the man ended up following behind.

The elevator lights indicated that the elevator was at the fourth floor, going down. They would have to wait awhile. In the light of the setting sun, shining in through windows on either side, the entire corridor gleamed like the inside of a well-greased cylinder. She peered around cautiously on both sides, then looked up at him with a conspiratorial smile; when she finally began talking, however, what she came out with was perfectly harmless and ordinary. Later she told him it had been a diversionary tactic for the benefit of hidden mikes.

"This is the center of the building. Both sides are exactly symmetrical. This whole side is partitioned off for the assistant director's own use. The other side used to be reserved for the director, but three years ago they converted his office and the meeting rooms and secretaries' offices into data storage centers.

The tapes alone take up an enormous amount of space. In another two or three years this part will be full, too."

"So the director moved somewhere else?"

She only leaned her head to one side, and didn't answer. The elevator came. As soon as she stepped inside, she pressed the red "capacity" light and gave a naughty laugh, wrinkling the skin above her nose. That way they would be able to go all the way to the second basement without stopping for other passengers.

(The recording breaks off again here. The tape counter reads 582. I'm sure the reason the horse kept trying to get me to finish the second tape, even calling up to see how I was doing and using supper as bait, was that he was after these few hours that went unrecorded. Naturally, I mean to tell everything. Surely she wouldn't be angry at me for that now.)

"The mikes don't work inside the elevator. If you have anything to say, say it now. We have this place to ourselves now but there isn't much time, so say it fast. Isn't there anything you want me to do? If not, then let me tell you something. I was raped by the chief."

She spoke so rapidly that when she had finished it was still only the ninth floor. He had no idea how to answer her. Perhaps the word "rape" isn't all that shocking in print, but heard spoken by someone directly involved, it was like gunpowder exploding in his ears.

His impression of her changed instantly. Gone without a trace were her haughty airs as the doctors' ally. Even her smooth, taut skin, that had seemed to him the mark of a fearless aggressor, now seemed to brand her as a victim. She kept her mouth tightly closed.

They stepped out into the employees' lobby. Except for the prevailing style of white coats and sandals and the smell of medicine, it was crowded enough to suggest the underground walkway of an office building at quitting time. Not surprisingly, considering she was the assistant director's private secretary, a number of people greeted her familiarly. Some glanced back and forth meaningfully at the two of them.

A pair of shaven-headed fellows in sweat pants came weaving through the crowd, ran up to her and stopped, bowing at sharp angles, then looked at her hopefully. With a practiced air she sent them casually on their way. Her self-assurance suggested that she must after all be on the doctors' side. Could he have heard mistakenly before, about the rape? Or was even rape treated differently here in the hospital from the way it was in ordinary society?

A barbershop, a notions counter, a travel bureau, a florist's shop, a coffee shop with chairs set out as far as the passageway, a speedy printing office, an electronic listening device store, a photo shop, a coin laundry, and then, as though glimpsed through a wide-angle lens, a steam-hazed dining hall.

In a far corner of the dining hall was an outsize television. Steel pipes had been assembled to a height of two meters off the floor, over which the table for the TV receiver jutted out sharply like a visor. Seating space in the blind spot underneath was particularly crowded. Granted there wasn't much on the tube worth watching around six o'clock, but still, why was such a noisy place so popular? For the very reason, it seemed, that it was so noisy: that made it a blind spot for hidden microphones, too.

Come to think of it, it did seem that everyone was snuggled unnaturally close together, as though whispering in each other's ears. A few couples were obviously engaged in romantic tête-à-têtes, but the majority seemed to be business partners huddled in confidential talks. As they walked between tables, a flurry rose wherever she went. Some couples even rose casually and left. The supervisor is never popular.

They sat down at the corner of a table for four, so close together that their knees almost touched; they had to sit that close just to be able to hear themselves talk. When the waiter came for their order she drew an A in the air with her finger, and then pantomimed pouring beer into a glass. There were five combination lunches on the menu, from A to E; today's A lunch was Chinese-style fried pork and vegetables, with corn soup. On television, a robot monster's scream marked the end of the children's program, and amber-colored lights flickered on the faces of surrounding diners as a commercial for an electronic mosquito-repellent device began.

"I was raped."

She whispered the words into the man's ear, then quickly faced forward again, tapping with her right forefinger on the white plastic tabletop. He knew he was being pressed for a response, but couldn't imagine what sort of answer she wanted. Was she trying to lodge a complaint with him against the chief, was she expressing solidarity with him as a fellow victim, or was she just seeking to arouse his sympathy?

Knowing that he was off target, he decided to give as noncommittal an answer as possible.

"When?"

She lowered her head and squirmed. He must have blown too hard in her ear. This time she blew back equally hard in his.

"Is it true about your wife being kidnapped in an ambulance?"

"If it weren't true, I wouldn't hang around this place so long, cutting work, would I?"

"I don't know about that."

"What do you mean?"

No matter how short their remarks, each one necessitated a shift from mouth to ear, then back from ear to mouth again; in the process everything they said took on a terribly suggestive sound.

"If you were a private eye, you'd have gone about looking for her quite differently, I bet."

"I've done everything a private eye could do. I've shadowed people, snooped around...."

"How many years have you been married?"

"Going on five."

"You still haven't done a survey of her general schedule, have you? Her circle of friends before you were married, her present associates. They say you can find all sorts of clues in

address books, calendar notations, and dog-eared pages in the
phone listings. You should check around with people in the
neighborhood, too. Did she have any set day in the week for
going out; if so, what hours was she gone and how was she
dressed and made up . . . ?"

"You don't realize—it's funny for me to be the one to say
this, but in the first place, I—"

"I know, you're a good-looking guy."

"That's not what I was going . . ."

The beer came. With her kneecap pressing against his like
a hard gumball as she urged him to share a toast, he could
hardly refuse. He glanced around. People's gazes flew off reluctantly in all directions, like flies chased away. The beer he
gulped down disappeared before ever hitting his stomach.

"What's your wife like?"

There was an unmistakable invitation in the pressure on
his knee. To ignore it would hurt her feelings, and at this stage
it would not be wise to earn her enmity. But if he took her up
on it, his own position in searching for his wife would lose all
credibility. He didn't know what to do.

"I have some pictures of her at home . . . when she was in
college she was in a district preliminary tryout for the Miss
Tokyo contest, so I've even got some big color pictures of her in
a bathing suit and stuff."

"You mean she's proud of her figure, and she's the flashy
type. Right?"

"That's not so."

"How come, I wonder."

"How come what?"

"I wonder if being married to a man makes him protective
like that."

He stole a careful look at her expression. There was no
trace of the sarcasm often accompanying that sort of remark,
which struck him as all the more reason to stay on guard.
While he searched for an answer, she went right on talking,
oblivious.

"There's something I think you ought to know." She
stared into his eyes, slurping down the rest of her beer through

pursed lips as if using an invisible straw. "Nobody really gives a hoot about you and your problems at all."

That was more than likely so. But it made him feel no better to be told so straight out like that. An unpleasant, clammy sensation oozed from his pores, as though he were a sponge being trampled underfoot. His hopes cracked and peeled off like a thin layer of ice on a frozen orange.

"But people from outside hardly ever get to go in there, do they, that room where you listen to the tapes? . . ."

"Just because something is hard to come by doesn't necessarily mean it's useful, does it?"

It was a suggestive warning. What was she after? Was this harassment, a frame-up, or just good will? But good will, like things that are hard to come by, wasn't necessarily useful. He was all too accustomed to demonstrations of good will from strangers by now.

Two A lunches were brought on aluminum trays. Instead of answering, he quickly took a mouthful of soup and discovered that he was so hungry he could scarcely taste it. For a while they busied themselves chewing. Finally, when the pile of fried pork and vegetables had been reduced to little more than broth, she glanced at her watch, then impulsively stuck out her wrist toward him, laughing with her eyes. A red scar three centimeters long ran parallel to her watchband.

The man's imagination spun. This must have some connection with that rape incident she had already mentioned twice now. Was she trying to arouse his sympathy by hinting at a past suicide attempt? His first impression had been that she and the chief of security worked in close harmony, but it could be that they didn't get along as well as they seemed to. Perhaps they were playing a dangerous game, one victim and the other aggressor. She had gone out of her way to show him an opportunity to press his advantage; it was up to him to make good on it.

She was first to take the next move.

"Do I seem unhappy to you, or happy?"

"You don't seem especially unhappy."

"Why not?"

Apparently he had said the wrong thing. If he had said that she seemed unhappy, that would have been a tacit admission that each of them had something to offer the other.

"It's just the impression I had, that's all. . . ."

She gave a slight smile, curling her upper lip, then abruptly shoved back her chair and stood up.

"Want to stop by my room on the way back?"

Half rising, he hedged.

"Would there be some advantage in that?"

A sharp pain shot through his anklebone. She had kicked him with the toe of her sandal. The skin was broken, and it was bleeding.

"Do you have to always just think about yourself like that? It's disgusting."

"Can I help it?"

She started walking ahead without looking back. He patted his ankle with the paper napkin he had used to wipe his mouth, then followed after her, weaving through the narrow spaces between tables and trying to let the pain of his injury drown his rising anger. She was like a spoiled baby monkey. What in hell gave her the right to act that way?

By the wall just outside the dining hall a crowd of twenty or so had gathered. That same shaven-headed twosome in sweat pants was in the act of beating up a middle-aged man in a doctor's white lab coat. They seemed to be the same pair as before, and yet they could just as easily have been different. The victim was seated on the floor, the front of his coat open, the buttons torn off. Blood streaming from his nose formed a spreading network across his undershirt, which was plastered against the flabby bulges of subcutaneous fat in his belly. One shaven-headed fellow, with a puffy face like a steamed bun, snatched off the victim's glasses and crushed them underfoot. His accomplice, who had one staring glass eye, kept jabbing his knee into the victim's nose, which had already been transformed into a ripe purple grape. Yet nobody made any move to intervene. Perhaps some special circumstances dictated against interfering.

The steamed bun saw the secretary; putting his hands up behind his ears, he flapped them like elephant ears. The glass eye smiled, showing even white teeth. She spoke to neither one in particular.

"Say the multiplication table."

The steamed bun pursed his lips proudly and popped his cheek with one finger, making a noise like tapping on the mouth of a bottle. He began to recite in a singsong.

"Two times two is four, two times three is six, two times four is eight, two times five is ten, two times six is twelve . . ."

The onlookers averted their eyes and stood stiffly and awkwardly. Everyone wore a cross, sulky look. It was not clear if their displeasure was aimed at the woman, at the two men, or at the victim himself. Meanwhile the glass eye kept his one good eye glued suspiciously on the man, who felt as ill at ease as if he were being forced to crap in public.

Without waiting for the recitation of the multiplication table to end, she began to walk away. The man followed behind her somewhat reluctantly. They left by a different route than they had come by. Gradually the lighting fixtures grew fewer and farther between, and the stores and coffee shops gave way to closed doors that looked like offices or storerooms. Every time they rounded another corner of the mazelike underground passage, the number of people diminished visibly, until finally they came to the foot of a narrow, deserted stairway. She turned around suddenly and spoke.

"What do you want?"

He felt he had fallen into a trap.

"I thought you were showing me the way, so I . . ."

"The way where?"

"I'd get lost by myself."

She tilted her head and smiled. He had no alternative but to continue following. They came out in the open air, and turning, he saw the main building of the hospital soaring up into deep violet clouds in the evening sky. Piled up in the dingy lamplight were hundreds of bicycles, wheels and handlebars intertwined. She pulled one out seemingly at random and started riding. The man ran alongside her. Now the jump shoes could show their stuff. As long as he wasn't up against a professional racer, he could hold his own against a bicycle for a good kilometer with no trouble. She looked back, saw him following closely behind as though in a dream, and increased her speed still more. The hem of her uniform fluttered in the wind, and her bare legs, fully revealed, stroked through the darkness.

They moved along a weed-grown path between row after row of wooden two-story buildings. These must be the wards for long-term patients that he had seen on the way to the assistant director's office, after the emergency doctor's accident. Stalks of gladioli mowed down by the bicycle wheels pointed downhill, their flowers the color of dried blood. She slammed on the brakes, and the man barely managed to avoid a collision. A three-story ferroconcrete building stood blocking the way ahead. It was a rather old-fashioned building, with vines covering its blue-gray walls, and red bricks framing its windows. This must once have been part of the main hospital buildings. Hanging there now was a wooden sign, smudged with ink, identifying it as SPECIAL WARD—CARTILAGE SURGERY.

The man was secretly relieved that it was not the woman's room. For the time being, then, he was on suspended sentence.

(7:43. The darkness outside my window rolled back and cracks between the clouds shone brightly, followed three seconds later by thunder and the spattering of large drops of rain. The horse should be here pretty soon. The tape counter still reads 582. I know he isn't going to like that. Rain is blowing in the window, and a foul green stench has begun to fill the room. Please, let this insanity end soon!)

He crossed a narrow driveway and pushed open the heavy front door with his shoulder, coming into a spacious hallway like a waiting room. The odor of disinfectant stung his nostrils, and the hum of ventilating fans crawled along the floor. He sensed the presence of people, but saw no one. Panting hard, the secretary opened the collar of her uniform and fanned herself. The man, also panting, wiped the sweat from his throat.

She turned, facing the elevator next to the front stairs as she spoke.

"Wait here. I'll talk to the assistant director and get a key to the room for you."

"Room? What room?"

She looked back sharply, stretched out both her arms, the fists tightly clenched, and stamped the floor impatiently with her sandal.

"I won't do anything to hurt you, so just do as you're told. You can save a whole lot of time by staying here at the hospital instead of always going back and forth between here and your house, right?"

She could say what she liked, but he still intended to go home. The reason there had been no answer on the phone before might very well be because his wife had been out running around in search of him. Besides, for all he knew, he might come upon some unexpected clue in the back of a bureau drawer. But there was no point in arguing about it with her. It was only common sense for someone lost to keep from acting blindly, and save strength for when the fog lifts. Silently he watched her disappear inside the elevator, and then seated himself on a narrow wooden bench covered with black vinyl. He was tired to the bone. The job of discriminating among those six sound tracks, all simultaneously bombarding him with random noises, had been far more grueling than he had realized.

Drowsiness fell on him like the dropping of a curtain. Just before drifting off to sleep, he thought he heard a voice like a slender whisper calling to him from somewhere upstairs. He dreamed. In his dream he washed his hands with a wormy bar of soap that was full of holes, and then his hands were full of holes, too. He rolled off the bench and woke up.

His awakening was so sudden that he had no clear sense of the passing of time. It could have been only a moment or two, or it could have been hours. Filled with a senseless fear that the secretary had gone off and left him, he leaped to his feet. He was also impatient to go back to the security room and wrestle with those tapes again. He must have hit his left elbow when he fell off the bench; his arm was numb from there to his little finger.

Beside the elevator, a hallway stretched back into the building. Only a blue emergency light was dimly shining. The lights were out behind the doors on both sides of the corridor. He tiptoed up the stairs and came to a smoking area with a framed color photograph of two mating horses hung on the wall. Compared with the painting in the assistant director's office, here the sexual organs were larger, and the overall impression was more scientific. Straight ahead, at chest height, were oblong glass doors; beyond them every corner was so brightly lit that there were no shadows, but he saw no sign of human beings. Papers, stainless-steel and glass instruments, rubber tubes and medicine bottles, and all manner of painful-looking equipment lay scattered across a desktop; immediately he recognized it as a nurses' station.

On the right were double wooden doors, and beyond them a corridor whose wooden floor was stained with oil. The wainscoting was painted in dark red horizontal stripes; where it ended was a door, from under which light was leaking out. He tried knocking but there was no answer. Mentally preparing a suitable excuse, he opened the door a crack. A young girl was lying in bed in a large room.

The girl lifted her head from her pillow, and her eyes met his. He started to back out, but something in her inquiring look, as though she had been half expecting him, made him stop.

"Not yet . . . please . . ."

She pleaded with him in a pastel powdery voice. Probably his uniform had aroused some misunderstanding; a patient familiar with hospital routine might well recognize that it belonged to security. But the girl's lips were smiling. It was an innocent, irregular smile, transparent as a tomato skin.

"I'm not going to do anything."

The man held his hands out palms-up by his shoulders to show her he meant no harm.

"But Daddy sent you, didn't he?"

As she spoke she shifted her gaze to the chair by the bed, as though her father sat there invisibly.

"I just looked in because the light was on. Maybe you can help me. I'm looking for the assistant director. . . ."

The girl returned her gaze to the man. Now her smile spread to the corners of her eyes.

"Listen—really, I still get dizzy when I walk."

"Who is your father, anyway?"

"As if you didn't know."

"Do you know who I am?"

"No."

She might not be just any patient, he thought. Her room was considerably bigger than the average patient's room, and well cared for. The bed seemed to be a special-order one, and the blanket had a nice thick nap. The curtains were not regulation white cotton but ivory-colored nylon. That smell of scalded milk seemed to come from the girl's own body. The man felt his heart suddenly weaken. Perhaps the smell reminded him of his wife.

"I wonder who your father could be, if he's somebody I'm supposed to know."

The girl pointed again to the chair beside the bed, and pursed up her lips. At first he assumed she was vaguely indicating somebody or other who often came and sat there. But when he traced the line of her finger, which was pointing at an odd angle, it seemed that she was directing his attention to a specific place on the chair leg. With the noise of fingers snapping in his mind, it hit him. If his security uniform meant to her that he knew her father, then there was only one possibility: the chief of security.

He acted on reflex, lifting up the chair and turning it over. Sure enough, the bottom of one leg had been hollowed out, and a small FM transmitter inserted. He removed the batteries and dropped them into his pants pocket.

"How disgusting. Planting bugs on his own daughter."

"I know, isn't it?"

Her voice was animated, and an atmosphere bubbled up

around her as though someone had taken the top off a carbonated drink. Precisely because she was so used to being spied on, this novel experience was evidently exciting.

"What's the matter with you, anyway?"

Instead of answering, the girl half sat up, resting one elbow on her pillow, and smiled. As she twisted her body, one leg was exposed above the knee. She was much younger than he had first thought. She couldn't be more than fifteen or sixteen. The outline of her body under the blanket had fooled him into thinking she was more grown-up. With her arms and legs stretched out, she had seemed well past little-girlhood, but the look on her face, he saw now, was quite babyish. And the curve of her thigh was still immature.

"Does your father want to take you out of the hospital?"

"As if you didn't know."

The girl turned over, lying on her back, and drew her feet toward her, knees up. The blanket was stretched like a tent over her slightly parted knees. Keeping a watchful eye on him, she began to move her hand rhythmically under the covers. He couldn't exactly see it move, but from the way her shoulders shook and from the waves her elbow was making in the blanket, he could clearly imagine the rhythmic motions her wrist was making, like an insect's feelers. He was thrown off balance. The back of his face swelled up, bloated like waterlogged sand.

"Cut it out."

His voice was husky, as though there were a lid on his throat.

"But he says this is how I look the cutest."

"Who says so?"

"The doctor."

"You mean the assistant director?"

The girl laughed, wrinkling the wings of her small, well-shaped nose. Then she made a spit bubble between her puckered lips, and smeared it on the tip of a slender finger taken from between the covers.

"Hey, I said cut it out."

He snatched her hand away. The girl's saliva smeared on his wrist. He had meant well by taking out the electronic listen-

ing device, but it had only backfired against him. Beyond all
doubt, the chief of security had been listening in. If only he had
left the device in place, he wouldn't have opened himself to any
suspicion, and the girl probably would have behaved herself
better.

"Why?"

The girl's transparent skin reddened. All the expression in
her turned-down face ran into the left side, leaving her right eye
behind, an empty, blank hole.

"You don't have to do that. Even if he is a doctor."

"That's what Daddy says, too."

"He's right. Why should anyone make you do something
you don't want to do?"

"I want to, though."

"Liar."

"But that picture in the frame, that's supposed to be the
doctor and me."

"What picture?"

"The one in the waiting room. You know, where the
horses are doing you-know-what."

She giggled. Maybe she was a little off her rocker. In a
flash, while he wasn't looking, she slipped her hand back under
the covers.

"Will you stop it?"

"Really you want to look, though, don't you?"

"How old are you?"

"Thirteen."

While she spoke, as though testing him, she began moving
her hand slowly toward the space between her knees, like a slug
crawling to its nest. She seemed to think she was making some
kind of a deal with him. Whoever had trained a kid of thirteen
to act like that ought to be shot. There was no excuse for it. He
had to admit, though, that behind his distaste and anger lurked
an emotion akin to jealousy. The girl did have an undeniable
fragility. But what gave an impotent middle-aged man like that
the right to take this sensation like freshly squeezed orange
juice, and dissipate it in such a filthy way?

The girl's hand stopped moving, as though she had seen and understood his anger.

"If I stop, will you promise not to take me away?"

He had never intended any such thing. If not for his own urgent situation, though, he felt it might not be such a bad idea at that, as long as he was under suspicion anyway. She did not seem to have much to carry with her, and all the talk about "take-outs" was an added incentive. On her bedside stand were a wash basin, a glass cup printed with strawberries, a pink-handled toothbrush, a tube of toothpaste, and a gaudily colored comic magazine; inside would be sanitary cotton, nail clippers, cream lotion, and the like. The blanket seemed to be hers, too, so if everything were wrapped up in it, there would be only one bundle to carry. The man stared into space from behind half-closed lids. He thought he would try putting on a little show for her benefit. He would pretend he had finally agreed to her deal after much thinking and hesitating, and that way settle the score in his favor.

He gave a slow and reluctant nod.

The girl bit her lower lip and laughed with an alarming innocence. She jumped up like a fish. The blanket fell away, and the front of her pajamas came open. The nipples of her just-swelling breasts were sunken, as though hiding in fright at the passage of time. She stretched an arm and pointed over his shoulder at the opposite wall. Her armpit was as white as the inside of a clamshell. The smell of scalded milk filled the room.

"If you're thirsty, there's some Coke in the fridge."

A green curtain with a woven pattern hung just the width of the doorway. He had assumed it was there only to hide, say, a sink, but instead he found himself in a small room complete with shower and gas burners. A small refrigerator was crammed with oranges, melons, and papayas in an array of color that seemed well suited to such a childish whore. Pulling out a bottle of Coke, he noticed a ladder beside the doorway. It was made of wood, attached vertically to the wall, and led straight up to an opening in the ceiling. Gazing up, he saw a weak light streaming out from overhead.

He had a fairly good notion of what that secret passageway might be for. Banging the Coke bottle against the wall as if he were having trouble opening it, he started up the ladder. The first rung creaked slightly, but after that he was able to ascend noiselessly. The opening led into a narrow space about one meter square. Boards overhead moved when his head brushed against them. It might be a trapdoor. On the side where the ladder was, that is, looking directly over the girl's room, there was a peephole about ten centimeters long and five millimeters wide. The light was coming from there.

He did not immediately grasp the implications of what was taking place inside. (Only now, writing it down, can I even put it into words; it was all I could do then to make myself believe what I saw.)

Close at hand were the calves of a woman. He could have reached out a hand and touched them. She was bare-legged, but her skin shone like well-polished furniture. He shifted his angle of vision and saw the heel of her sandal grinding into the floor. It was the secretary. Beyond her were two beds. The peephole was too low to obtain a good view, but he could just make out two men lying on them. One was the emergency doctor who had fallen from the second-floor window in the midst of masturbating, and landed unconscious; the other was the assistant director. The emergency doctor was lying face up, naked, his penis as erect as ever. Perhaps it was only the man's imagination, but its color seemed slightly bluish compared with that afternoon.

The assistant director was lying with his back to the doctor. He had on a white shirt, and was naked from the waist down. His penis lay limply against one thigh, looking exactly like fish entrails.

A web of dozens of narrow cords, weaving in and out among each other, bound the two men together by the hips. The ends of the cords were fastened to their skins with color-coded adhesive tape and connected to a machine set up between the beds. One nurse was staring at the machine, making notations, while another, shaking drops of oil from a bottle, was busily massaging the doctor's penis with the rhythmic sound of a stray cat lapping milk. The assistant director had deep creases between his eyebrows; from time to time he would say "N thirteen," "K fourteen," or some such thing, flexing and unflexing one finger raised in the air in sign. The nurse in charge of the machine would respond by manipulating dials or adjusting the position of the adhesive tape; the nurse in charge of the penis would slow down or speed up her motion.

How could he have expected any help from this crowd in looking for his wife? They were like a bunch of worm-eaten dolls escaped from a junkman's truck, having an insane party.

(Later I found out that they were then in the midst of a bizarre experiment, attempting to translate the sensations in the doctor's continuously erect penis into electrical signals, and then transmit those to the assistant director's cerebrum, thereby enabling him to reach a complete orgasm simultaneously with the doctor's ejaculation.)

"Attention, visitor in room eight on the second floor. Attention, visitor in room eight on the second floor. Entering patients' rooms without permission is prohibited. Please report at once to the nurses' station. Please report at once to the nurses' station. Attention, visitor in room eight . . ."

The voice of a middle-aged woman, shrill and distorted by a small speaker, yet bearing a certain professional menace, called from the foot of the ladder. The girl was laughing as she made some reply. The assistant director and the others beyond the peephole also reacted instantaneously. The voice over the speaker must have sounded not only in the girl's room, then, but over all the building.

His eyes met those of the nurses. The secretary's calves changed position. In reflex he covered the hole with his left hand.

Sharp pain . . .

He slid down the ladder. She had stabbed his palm with a

sharp pin or something, and a drop of blood had formed. The crazy bitch. He put his mouth over the stab wound and sucked on it as he made his way back to the girl's room.

With one arm under her pillow, the girl was beaming triumphantly. Her other arm was swaying like a narrow-stemmed flower over her head. In her hand was an imitation lily, just like the real thing, its head drooping heavily; attached behind it was an intercom speaker. Then had his entire conversation with the girl been overheard after all? What sort of things had they said? This was worse than the hidden microphone, because this way their identities were known.

Before he could recover, a noise came from the adjoining room with the ladder. It sounded like the creaking of a poorly fitted door. His hand hurt. He prepared to run away. Someone might be coming after him. On the one hand, he felt that he had done nothing to be ashamed of, yet for some reason he was prompted by a sense of conspiratorial guilt.

(A certain scenario just suggested itself to me.

After the transmitter batteries were removed and his ears thus effectively stopped, the chief of security must have been frustrated. He immediately contacted the nurses' station and had them switch on the wired intercom.

He was able to monitor everything then until the man went into the adjoining room to get a Coke.

At that point conversation ceased, and an unnaturally long silence began. It hadn't been very long, in fact, but the suspicion-tormented chief, unable to control himself, had gone ahead and ordered the warning broadcast.

For a man who was father to a thirteen-year-old sex maniac, it was probably the most natural step in the world.)

All at once the girl started to meow like a cat. She swung one leg farther out and stuffed the twisted-up blanket in her crotch. Her legs, like long pieces of spaghetti, may have been lacking in femininity, but they seemed so clean he wanted to lick them. Her round rump, encased in charcoal-gray pants, had the power of a magnet, urging awakening to the sense of touch in his palms.

That meowing, however, was a bit out of place. Was that something else that the assistant director had taught her? It gave him a quick pain to imagine her acting out the part of a cat in heat for that man.

"I'll come by again real soon."

There was a tenderness, surprising even to him, in his voice. Maybe once his wife was safely located and things had calmed down a bit, he might really be able to do that.

When he stepped out into the hall there was the noise of doors slamming shut. A few figures dressed in pajamas raced toward their rooms, too late. They must have been patients who had heard the broadcast a few minutes before and came to see what was going on. They looked like nothing so much as hermit crabs frightened off by footsteps.

The nurses' station was as empty as before. The broadcasting room must be somewhere else. The door was ajar. It couldn't hurt to stop off for a few minutes. At this point it would serve no purpose if he did head off the secretary and get back to the waiting room first. Besides, they had stopped him from looking in on the scene of the experiment. It was more important now to try to find some disinfectant for his wound. It was small, but puncture wounds were more prone to infection than incisions, he had heard.

Half the back wall was taken up by racks of patients' charts, alphabetically arranged. He searched for his wife's without finding it. He had not really expected it to be there, so he was not disappointed.

Now he was sorry that he hadn't found out the girl's name. Maybe it wasn't too late to go back and ask her. He did know her room number, though; it was room eight on the second floor. Surely there were some records arranged by room number around somewhere.

He was searching the top of a big office desk, which was placed in the center of the room so that it could be used from either side, when from behind a pile of papers he heard the sound of water being poured out of a narrow jug.

A giggle, then the white cap of a nurse appeared. She must have been a head nurse or the equivalent, judging from the three black stripes edging her cap. A black mole stood out by her nose. The sound of running water stopped. She remained squatted down with no sign of getting up, so he went around for a look, and found her straddling a low, round seat just off the floor. She sat facing a private, low workbench filled with miniature broadcasting equipment.

"Caught me, didn't you?"

"I'd like to know what's wrong with the patient in room eight."

"I'm sorry." The head nurse dug the tip of her ballpoint pen into a hole in the side of the bench and smiled, her lower jaw slack and heavy. "If I'd known you were from security, I never would have made that announcement."

There was unmistakable respect in the eyes she turned on his uniform. This fresh reminder of the security room's power only increased his uneasiness.

"Who'd you think I was?"

"They come all the time, people who've gone bananas after listening to those tapes, wanting her for a take-out. . . ."

"What tapes?"

"Her tapes. I don't see what's so great about that voice of hers; sounds like a cat with the hiccups to me. But to each his own. Look at the assistant director—he turns to jelly when he listens to them."

"You mean her father sells them? . . ."

"But I wonder how they sniff her out. After all, it's not as though he spelled out just who she is."

"Is she really sick?"

"Oh, she's sick, all right. Why, just the other day, after someone took her out, she'd shrunk eighteen centimeters by the time she came back a couple of days later."

"She shrinks?"

"It's a terrible disease called osteolysis. The bones dissolve. Are you hurt?"

"It's okay."

He moistened a smear of dry blood on his wrist with his tongue, and wiped it off on his sleeve.

"Now, now—let's have a look."

The sound of water spilling began again. It was somewhere close by. He could see no tipped-over bottles or cups in particular. The head nurse stiffened her body and looked up at him, the corners of her eyes reddening slightly.

"What's that?"

"I'm peeing." She lifted up her skirt over her hips, and there, underneath the crack in her big bottom like a machine-stitched seam, was an enamel bedpan surrounded by sponges. "My bladder's sphincter muscle doesn't work. It won't follow orders."

"That must be inconvenient, when you have to move around. . . ."

"You can say that again. Right now on the third floor here they're doing some kind of interesting experiment. Everybody else went off to look and left me here all by my lonesome . . . not that I really am lonesome . . . exactly. I can't very well diaper myself. I sweat a lot. For heaven's sake, do you have to keep staring like that?"

Despite what she said, she kept up a nasal tittering and made no move to drop her skirt back down, so he couldn't help watching as droplets of urine turned to bubbles skating around on the surface.

"Maybe I'll go have a look at that experiment on the third floor, too."

"There's cold beer in the refrigerator."

The man smiled and declined it with a wave of his hand, then turned and walked out as fast as possible without offending her.

In the center of the waiting room stood the secretary, legs slightly apart. Her weight was distributed evenly on both feet, as though she were waiting to confront the enemy. The light coming from behind put her head in shadow, making the outline of her hair indistinguishable and her round face even rounder-looking. She had one finger stuck through her key ring, and was shaking it in a circle, pointed at her chest. The steel keys shone as they spun around.

(There's the car. Finally, the horse is here to pick me up.)

Notebook Three

I am in an underground room in the old hospital grounds. Last night's rain is over, and dazzling afternoon sunshine is pouring in through cracks in the ventilator. I just now decided to start writing again, using a cardboard box for a desk. I don't know how much longer I will be able to keep on with it. When the sun goes down it won't be worth continuing, and if my pursuers track down this hideout, the game will be up.

With this third volume, the meaning and aim of these notes have undergone a complete change. The other two were ordered by the horse, but this time I have no client. That means I don't have to hold anything back or feel any constraints; it also means I don't have to lie to protect myself any more. No matter how I may end up offending the horse, after all, I can't be any worse off than I am already. This time, for sure, I will make a clean breast of everything. If the other two notebooks were reports, what I am about to write is an indictment. I have no idea yet whom I can possibly get to read it, but in any case I don't want to sit idly by and let them get away with this.

Just beyond the cardboard box, with the blanket twisted between her thighs, breathing softly in her sleep, is the little girl from room eight. The smell of scalded milk is gone, however, having lost out to the acrid stink of rat urine. Sounds of fireworks and an electric guitar band, advertising the anniversary eve party, scheduled to begin in six hours, echo back and forth through this underground labyrinth, pulsating like weird sighs. I thought I heard sounds of human voices muttering and snickering mixed in with the reverberations, but it could just be that my nerves are starting to go.

Anyway, I will pick up where I left off in notebook two.

Last night, when the horse came as agreed to take him out for a late meal, the man made no attempt to cover his irritation. No sooner had they climbed into the white van than the sky burst open and it began to rain. The front windshield was covered by a sheet of water, and the wipers were useless. The horse bent over the wheel in silence, while the man silently rubbed his temples with his fingertips. He had been writing continuously since that morning, and his nerves were as rusted out as old telephone wires. The horse had been nearly two hours late in coming, and by now his energy pills were starting to wear off.

"Where are we going?"

"I thought my place, so we could relax."

A gust of wind blew at smoldering ashes, igniting them into sudden flames. After behaving all along as though he had no private life whatever, here the horse was suddenly inviting the man home with him. The man felt a wave of curiosity, tempered by caution. He gave a huge yawn, tears spilling from his eyes.

It was such a terrible downpour that it's hard to say exactly where they went or how they got there. They went down a long slope and then back up, but it could have been that they took a long detour and ended up at a different place somewhere on the same elevation that the hospital is on. If so, it was probably the west end. The road along the cluster of wooden infirmaries stops in front of the cartilage surgery building, and of course traffic can go no farther. Beyond lie the foundations of the old demolished hospital building, buried in head-tall weeds and entangled like some ancient ruin in tree branches, with here and there a glimpse of an entryway underground; this hideout is in óne of the rooms below ground. Farther on lies a huge, shapeless plot of parched land, as big as three baseball fields combined, on which stands the old target range where the horse works out. Once when I was crossing that vacant lot to take the horse something to eat, I tilted my head in surprise when, off in the distance, across the roof of the target range, I saw a structure like a many-faceted piece of sculpture glittering like a jewel in the morning sun. That grove on the cliff overlooking the sea was certainly an excellent choice for the new residential area.

Standing on a lawn swollen like green gelatin as it sucked light from the overhead street lamps was an apartment building made of glass and ivory-colored tiles, like a work of abstract art. Each floor had a deep veranda, so that the building became progressively narrower toward the top, like a small pyramid. Abandoning the van in an outdoor parking lot, they ran to the entrance, where an automatic door made of glass a centimeter thick slid noiselessly open, revealing a light-blue-gray wall-to-wall carpet so thick they padded across it like cats.

The horse's apartment was on the top floor.

Opening the door, they stepped immediately into a large sitting room. Beyond the glass window that took up the entire wall facing them spread darkness, etched with scratch-like lines of rain. On either side of the window were odd light fixtures, or more precisely, a pair of life-size acrylic resin sculptures that radiated light from either end.

Both side walls had a door near the entrance that led into an adjoining room; one wall was covered by a glass-doored cabinet, and the other with elaborate stereo equipment and a huge color photograph. The subject of the photo was another horse, a stallion rearing on his hind legs, with his erect organ in full frontal view; for a room decoration it was a little too scrupulous in detail.

By the window was a round table of polished lavender marble, on top of which sat a lacquered tray; over the tray lay a dark blue cloth patterned with white fish. The room's chairs, wallpaper, and rugs were all done in the same ivory color, with a pattern of tiny blue-green flowers. On paper the décor may sound elegant, but in reality it was rather desolate. The paint on the window frame was cracked and discolored; a flower vase on the ledge wore a shawl of dust around its shoulders; padding stuck out through a rip in the back of one of the chairs. The room seemed to embody the slothful sort of bachelorhood often left behind in the wake of a careening, drunken-driving sort of married life.

The horse gruffly offered him a beer, lifting back the blue cloth. Expensive-looking cakes of raw fish and rice decorated with real bamboo leaves were arranged radially in a circle.

"Well, how are you coming with the investigation?"

The man did not reply. Before handing over the notebook,

he wanted a satisfactory explanation of the footsteps recorded on the beginning of the first cassette. If the horse had not attached some special significance to them, he would not have included that segment on the tape in the first place.

The horse nodded soothingly in short, quick nods.

"There's lots of time. Never mind that. What's more important is that the first notebook you gave me yesterday seems to have found its way into your wife's hands somehow."

"Then you've found her?"

"Not quite. It's been left to a liaison man."

"If you know how to contact her, then you must be able to find out where she is! I'll do it myself if you'll just introduce me to the liaison."

"You can't rush these things." The horseradish in his rice cake must have been too strong; he coughed out air from his mouth that he had breathed in through his nose. "You can't try to force them. Put the other side on its guard, and you've lost all advantage."

"If you would just try, there must be any number of ways of going about it!"

In place of an answer the horse switched subjects, launching into an explanation of the meaning of the opening part of that tape.

"Ah yes," he began, "it was on the morning of the day I first asked my secretary to make those tapes, which would put it right around the day before yesterday. With the hospital's founding anniversary just around the corner, a special meeting of the council had been called, and while there I happened to catch some promising news. At the exact moment when your wife was supposedly brought in by ambulance, evidently a theft took place in the outpatient pharmacy. It wasn't too much of a theft, actually; a glass window facing the courtyard was smashed, and some fever-reducing and sleep-inducing medicines were taken, along with a supply of contraceptive pills valued at about eight hundred thousand yen. That was all. Hardly worth mentioning under ordinary circumstances. Not that thefts are an everyday affair around here, mind you. On the contrary, most people agree that the hospital's internal crime rate is extremely low. Of course, depending on what you want to call a crime, the rate goes either up or down. By adopting the standard concept, you could even argue that the hospital is a regular hotbed of crime. But when a person finally becomes a patient, all his preconceived ideas are powerfully affected. And as his preconceived ideas undergo alteration, inevitably so does his view of crime. Where there is no victim, you see, of course there can be no aggression.

"The reason that the pill theft was taken up so carefully on that particular day, however, was that those pills were a new morning-after type. Everybody's been talking about them in connection with a special competition on the program for the anniversary eve party, that's going to decide which woman has the most and the longest orgasms. Excitement has been running high ever since the first announcement was made; rumor has it that quite a number of patients have secretly equipped themselves with pills in order to enter the contest, and are practicing enthusiastically to be ready.

"Well, as soon as I heard that report, I had a flash of intuition. It couldn't have been mere chance that the time and place of those two incidents, your wife's disappearance and the burglary in the pharmacy, coincided so perfectly. If your wife had had some form of contact with the pill thief, then that would explain everything. Because, to be perfectly candid, up until then it didn't seem to me that her disappearance deserved to be treated as much of an event. The only possible explanation, I felt, was that she had had the help of someone inside the hospital, with whom everything had been arranged beforehand. So either you were lying or else your wife had pulled a fast one on you. . . . Whichever it was, I couldn't bring myself to take the whole thing seriously."

"Then how come you let me have a room of my own, and gave me free access to all the tapes from the security room?"

"I wasn't the one who wanted to keep you around."

"Who was, then?"

"My secretary."

"What for?"

"She doesn't give up easily, that's why. When she decides she wants something, she isn't satisfied until she's gotten it."

"Isn't she a little strange?"

"You just happen to be the type she goes for."

"One time she kicked me in the leg so hard it started to bleed, and another time she stuck me in the palm of the hand with a needle, and one other time she bit me so hard in the arm I thought she was going to tear a chunk right out."

"She's a test-tube baby."

"So?"

"So she's completely alone in the world, that's all."

"You don't mean she's a synthetic human being or anything, do you?"

"Her mother was already dead. She grew from a ripe egg extracted just after the woman died. Her father was one cc of mixed semen borrowed from the semen bank. So she has no familial feelings whatsoever. Her sense of human relationships, shall we call it, is entirely missing."

"Sounds pretty creepy."

"For example, the sense of loneliness is one manifestation of the nesting instinct, they say. And skin sensations, it seems, are at the root of all feelings and emotions. While she, you see, has no nest or roots to go back to, at all."

"That's not my fault."

"It isn't hers, either. Anyway, she probably has a hard time understanding it: why you run around frantically searching for your wife while she has to sit and cool her heels waiting."

"She's got a lot of nerve; this has nothing to do with her!"

"Still, it's probably hard for her to understand."

The horse drank down the rest of his beer and uncapped a new bottle as he continued talking.

Five years ago, he had taken charge of a certain experiment. More accurately, it had been a plan of his, or rather of his estranged wife's (the Psycholinguistics Center employee). The experiment was entitled "Sexual Arousal and Inhibition Induced by Symbolic Representation," and in simple terms its goal had been quantification of the various mechanisms by which sexual acts reduced to symbols (pornography, tapes, etc.) might affect observers or listeners. In addition to ordinary people attracted by the daily remuneration, participants had included a select group of patients chosen by recommendation from each department, all suffering from rare diseases involving sensual dysfunction. I will omit details, since they have little bearing on the matter at hand, but in the end it became clear that vocal stimulation had particularly outstanding evocative powers, unmatched by those of any other kind of symbolic representation. In humans the sense of smell is underdeveloped and the sense of sight overdeveloped, so it was the sense of hearing, on a plane midway between the two, that seemed to function most effectively of all.

She, the secretary, had been one of the specially selected participants. And she alone had reacted in a completely different way from all the others, throwing the experimental results into confusion. Of course, all the participants' responses varied to some extent, but in the main they followed certain fixed rules, with discrepancies never exceeding the bounds permissible for individual differences. She alone had had no reaction whatever. Worse, she had actually shown negative physiological reactions: when forced to sit and listen, she would develop a neck rash, or visual difficulties.

Actually, the original purpose of the experiment had been to find a treatment for the horse's stubborn impotence. Since he had no underlying physical problems, some form of outside stimulus was believed responsible. The Psycholinguistics Center was working on his case; the horse was thus in the awkward position of being simultaneously a doctor in his own right and a patient of his estranged wife's. The name of his disease, it was discovered, was "traumatic interpersonal relations neurosis." There was some hope that greater anonymity in his interpersonal relations might provide effective treatment. Therefore it was predicted that if properly prescribed, tapes recorded by hidden microphone should have a positive effect, given their high degree of anonymity. Results had been largely as expected.

To have one such glaring exception, though, even granted it was only one out of many, spoiled the otherwise consistent results.

They had decided to try applying direct stimulation to her pleasure center. The response had been normal. She had even had a short but strong orgasm, accompanied by uterine spasms. Like the horse, she evidently suffered from no particular innate disability. It seemed to be another case of "traumatic interpersonal relations neurosis."

This similarity with the symptoms of the horse drew attention, and little by little the experiment came to focus solely on her. Some suspected that her case was further complicated by experiment hypersensitivity: having been raised in a test tube, she was an object of great curiosity, constantly sought after by people in all the research departments. To ease tension, the experiment was transferred to a room in a fashionable residential section, with a mound of drug-injected chocolates kept in a silver bowl on the table. Seeking a breakthrough, they had even hired an electrical engineer well versed in bugging techniques, in order to assemble data on a variety of sexual acts. By coincidence, he was the father of the long-term patient in room eight of the special-diseases ward in the cartilage surgery department. But, as if to mock all their efforts, not one of the needles on the instruments attached to her had ever shown the slightest motion.

One evening the experiment had dragged on late; she and the engineer had been left alone together, with the cries of an orgasm wafting out of the stereo and into the room. Carried away in perverted excitement, the engineer had raped her.

The night had been hot and sultry, about like tonight, and since she was wearing nothing but thin underwear, the rape was over with easily in just a few minutes. Smeared with blood, she had put up no real resistance, content to watch the engineer's actions intently without even raising her voice. Ever since, however, she had grown increasingly scornful of all kinds of sexual stimulation, a strong indication that the damage had been emotional as well as physical.

The matter was brought before the council. After inquiry,

opinion was agreed that her case merited further investigation, but that there was no sign of any crime involved. After all, she had not only yielded to the engineer unresistingly, but actually expressed a desire to continue the experiment with him. Therefore it was perhaps only natural to suspect her of harboring strong hopes that the experiment would provide a cure for her frigidity. Some members of the council went so far as to accuse her of wanting to be raped.

Respecting her own wishes, the council had entrusted her to the Psycholinguistics Center with a recommendation for long-term observation. The engineer, of course, could hardly protest. He had escaped the consequences of his crime, and moreover, he had begun to fall passionately in love with her.

The horse, however, had had private misgivings about it all. As a member of the council he had cast an affirmative vote, but that was no reflection of his true opinion. It made little sense for a daredevil of a woman like her, with a test tube for a mother, to be so cooperative. There had to be some underlying motive. What could she want so desperately that in order to get it she was willing to endure the anguish of working face to face with her own rapist? Something that belonged to him, perhaps, such as his technical skill. For such a young woman it seemed a shade too sly, but perhaps the tapes of sexual acts were a mere pretext, and her real interest lay in the general surveillance operation itself.

His instinct had been right on target. Before anyone realized it, the surveillance project had left the experiment behind and taken on a life of its own. It had continued to grow and proliferate, soon becoming so elaborate that it constituted a business in itself. She became the horse's secretary, and the electrical engineer became chief of security. In retrospect, it even seemed as though she might have secretly set the whole chain of events in motion on purpose.

(The girl from room eight turned over in her sleep. Maybe the light streaming in through the ventilator is too bright. I released the lock on the wheelchair and turned it facing a different way. She half-opened her eyes and smiled. I felt a peace like balancing on the point of a needle. When I put a finger up to her mouth she sucked on it noisily. The rain from last night which had soaked into the ground must have begun to evaporate; the air is heavy and suffocating. Today will be hot again.)

Incidentally, I have already said as much on several occasions, but the assistant director and the horse are, of course, one and the same. The horse is the end-product of the assistant director's philosophy that *a good doctor makes a good patient*. By hospital standards he is supposed to have acquired a whole new personality, but common sense tells me it doesn't even amount to the difference in myself before and after brushing my teeth. In short, since the assistant director was unable to make his own penis cooperate, he decided to borrow the lower half of some other man's body, have the sensations in that borrowed penis electrically transmitted to his own sex center, and thus experience sex vicariously. The weird experiment that I had observed through the hole in the ceiling of room eight in the cartilage surgical ward the first night after sneaking into the hospital (see notebook two for details) had been designed to achieve that purpose.

His vicarious experience had been even more successful than they had hoped. When I looked in, the still-unconscious emergency doctor had just had an ejaculation, thanks to the young nurse's massaging, and at the same time the assistant director had just had his very first orgasm; for a short time, he had even achieved an eighty-percent erection of his own. However weird, though, an experiment is only an experiment. Had that been all, probably nothing would have come of it. Weighted down with the urgent problem of my wife's disappearance, I had no time or mental energy to devote to other people's problems.

That same day, however, I heard about the assistant director's horse-man fantasy. Poor visibility does not mean total inability to see; it means only that something in the way can be seen too well. It was as though all sorts of colors of paint had been smeared over the lens of a telescope that was hard to see through to begin with.

It happened right where notebook two ends—just after the secretary got the key to the emergency doctor's room and led me half-forcibly to building E4. She came inside with me as though it were quite natural; indicating the nude photos around the bed with her chin, she broke the silence with a sudden, morose question.

"Of all these women, which one would you most like to see masturbating?"

I hesitated for an answer, but she pressed me further.

"I want to know which one's your type."

"That's an awfully sudden question . . . you must have the wrong idea about me. I just . . ."

"Did you hear the results of the X ray?" She quickly changed the subject. "It's a cranial fracture, they say, in the back of the head. . . . If he doesn't regain consciousness by the day after tomorrow, they say it'll be all over."

"I never dreamed it would come to such a thing. . . ."

"It's all right; anyway, he's still single. His only living relative is an aunt with Ménière's disease who works in the uniform factory. So tomorrow, if it looks like his condition is going to stay the same, they're going to chop it off."

"Chop what off?"

"Right about here." She made a sawing motion with her hand, in the vicinity of her navel. "They're going to cut him in two and use the lower half of his body for the assistant director's substitute penis."

"You're joking."

"The assistant director is on cloud nine."

"That must be against the law, a thing like that. . . ."

"Would you masturbate for me?"

"I beg your pardon?"

"It says in the Psycholinguistics Center's compatibility test that when you can imagine someone masturbating without feeling any aversion, then there will be an ideal union of mind and body."

"Are you serious?"

"I've never met anybody like that yet. I'd started to give up, but with you I have a feeling that I wouldn't mind watching a little."

"Well, I mind. The answer is no."

"Please? Why not, since I want you to?"

"Seriously, what are they going to do with just the lower half of his body?"

"Tie it on the back of the assistant director's waist so he'll look like a horse."

"A horse . . ."

"Come on, masturbate for me, please?"

"No!"

"Why not?"

I still could not understand her sadistic outbursts. They had to be deliberate spite, I thought, or else some sort of practical joke. Pleading the excuse that I wanted to listen to the tapes in the playback room awhile longer, I barely managed to make an escape. The substitute penis, the compatibility test—I could hardly believe any of it. All I knew was that I wanted to run far away from that terrible miasma, holding my nose.

But, as I have written many times already, the assistant director is in fact a horse-man.

Was the emergency doctor severed in two as the secretary predicted, then, and made into a horse's lower half?

As it happened, during that night the nurses had made the emergency doctor's penis into quite a plaything. A few actually attempted intercourse with it, but more often they would play with it, twisting it inside a vacuum cleaner hose or testing its hardness by seeing how many sheets of copy paper it could break through, until finally by morning it had become a bloody pulp, no longer usable. Some said there had been an instigator, but the facts were not clear. It was also rumored that it had been carried off by another department afterward, but no one knew exactly what had become of it.

Nevertheless, the assistant director is in fact a horse.

Therefore they must have stolen the lower half of someone else's body.

Actually, from the time I first began writing notebook one, the chief of security was already dead. Of course he was; nobody could stay alive, reduced to just his lower half. His top half was cremated the same day and buried respectfully in the hospital cemetery. In accordance with Buddhist ritual, he was given a posthumous name, and since he was a distinguished staff member a formal announcement of his demise was issued. To all appearances he died an eminently respectable death.

It was the afternoon of the second day. The assistant director had been staring dumfounded at the remains of the emergency doctor, so badly damaged by the nurses' horseplay that the essential part was beyond repair. Then all at once the body of the chief of security fell into his hands, with that enormous appendage of which its owner had been so proud (one can't deny he was justified; it measured 7.2 centimeters around and nineteen centimeters long, they say). The chief's only chronic disease had been mild epilepsy, and so, omitting an autopsy, they cut his body in two while it was still fresh. Special treatment was given to the open wound on the bottom half, and to this moment that half is being carefully preserved by life-sustaining equipment, so that the horse can use it at any time as an auxiliary lower body.

The question remains, can this incident legitimately pass as a simple death? Hospital terminology may have another term for it, I don't know, but in my book it's a clear case of murder. Police authority surely extends even to this place. If they want me to take the witness stand, I am ready anytime.

I had gone to the chief's office to exchange my old tape for a new one (the twenty-third). The chief was bent over the account books, totaling the week's sales. All at once five of those shaven-headed young fellows in sweat pants came rushing in without knocking. Four of them held his arms and legs while the fifth pushed a chair cushion against his face. Nobody said a word the entire time; the killing was done with utmost dexterity.

Just a couple of weeks before, an article in the paper had reported that smothering with pillows was now the preferred method of hired assassins. As soon as I realized it was my turn next, my much-vaunted muscles turned as stiff as dried sardines and refused to move. The men ignored me, however. One of them even gave me a conspiratorial wink, which only increased my discomfort. Spiritedly lifting up and carrying out the chief's body, they laid it on a wheeled bed waiting in the corridor, straightened the legs, and dashed off with it.

Immediately the phone rang. It was the secretary.

"That went very well."

"So it was you, after all. . . ."

"We've got to decide on his successor now. Do you want me to recommend you?"

From the other end of the receiver I could hear surging battle cries, like those of men rushing headlong into the depths of some midnight festival. She must have been calling from the basement security station. Perhaps the bunch carrying the body had arrived. She shouted something back in a tone of exasperation, and the line was cut off. It hadn't sounded like real exasperation so much as a kind of collusion, like a refusal already expected by both sides.

How on earth had she got them to do such a thing? She did have the personal motive of retaliation for the rape. It was a bit late for that, though, and hard to imagine that she could have won their sympathy all of a sudden after so much time. Or had something in the chief's everyday manner turned the men against him? With their sweat suits and close-shaven heads all alike, karate training, regimental behavior . . . if forced to do something against their will, they might very well mutiny. But to my knowledge, their rules of conduct were all devised by a young man acting as leader (a goiter patient, son of a hospital florist), without any outside interference. At first, I myself had taken the chief to be a standoffish type, the sort of person it's hard to feel at ease around. Now it seems to me that that was just a sign of the unsociability that tends to characterize most technical experts. Apart from maintenance control of the surveillance system and enlargement of the cassette sales organization, his sole concern in life had been somehow to curry favor with the secretary; in fact, he had seemed a man of awkwardly single-minded bent. Our acquaintance lasted barely two short days; more and more, I wish that I had got to know him better.

The chief's spring-equipped chair kept spinning gently and noiselessly around. In all honesty, I was frightened out of my wits. And when I discovered it wasn't the assistant director who was behind the deed, I was even more terrified. The poor little girl from room eight lies twitching the thin, dry skin over her lips as she murmurs voicelessly in her sleep; how can I ever explain to her the cruel fate her father has met? In any case, I am not under any circumstances going to let her near that assistant director, who's now a horse; nor is there any reason I should.

The horse scolded me for purposely stalling with the notebooks, and trying to gain time. Of course, that's what I want to do; there is no way I can take this crazy business and write it up without somehow incurring their displeasure. They may think they can make me write an alibi for the horse, but they have another think coming. I know a trick or two myself now.

Strange as it may sound, I can sense that at this moment I'm only a step away from complete control over the hospital. Early in the morning on the day after the murder, the council held an emergency session and unanimously chose me as the new chief of security. I haven't actually accepted the position yet, but since the secretary went ahead and put three black stripes back on my uniform, everybody thinks it's all settled, and I don't know what I can do about it. The electronic surveillance system has swollen to unmanageable, mammoth size, and continues to absorb new information all the time; even though no one is actually in charge of it any more, the mere suggestion that such a person might exist seems to inspire awe and submissiveness. Especially among patients, the idea seems to produce a certain masochistic sense of relief; reactions run the gamut, from those who make long, involved, self-damaging confessions into hidden microphones, to those who turn themselves into private radio stations by attaching FM transmitters to their bodies, and go around broadcasting sounds of themselves defecating or jerking off in public to the accompaniment of hoots and jeers. During the short time I spent seated by the playback equipment, less than seventy-two hours, I became familiar with hundreds of such regular patrons, male and female.

Not that I have figured out the best way to make use of this power. But if I wanted to, I'll bet I could have the entire hospital at my feet in a minute. My predecessor didn't seem particularly aware of this fact, but even in the hands of those who little deserve it, power is still power. Everyone tries to humor me now; all I have to do is turn the other way and keep my feelings under cover. Even the council has taken to giving me a copy of the discussion agenda beforehand. Informers and letters of apology come one on the heels of the other.

Today during lunch break at the dining hall entrance, one of the collectors gave me a hand-printed leaflet. A collector is a spy who goes around with a hi-fi FM receiver slung across his shoulder, looking for extra radio waves. It has become commonplace to fasten small FM transmitters to other people's eaves, beds, cosmetics cases, sandal heels, umbrella handles, and other places, so they are spread out fairly evenly across the hospital grounds; even so, depending on location and direction, some areas still escape the web of the security room's central administrative system—underground rooms of reinforced concrete with few openings, for example, or the shadows of special storehouses with walls of galvanized iron. Such places are favorite hunting spots for collectors. Even the late chief of security was a mere collector until the Psycholinguistics Center sought his help as a technical adviser; for a while, even after the experiment began he had contracts with four or five of the best collectors, and was accepting offers for tapes. Why is it, I wonder, when everybody listens on the sly, that collectors alone are treated like informers, and made the objects of such prejudice? Perhaps that is the other side of power.

The contents of the leaflet did not amount to much. On the top half was a line drawing of a black sphere covered with holes, with a human figure sticking its head into each hole. Centrifugal force seemed to be at work, since they were all floating with their bodies out radially in a most natural way.

People running, people typing, people squatting on the toilet, people busy making lace, people having coitus with their neighbors . . . the whole thing looked in a way like an old land mine, or like a collection of people all sharing the same huge head. Underneath was a string of sentences written in slogan style.

"Everyone is basically alone. Are you afraid of good health? Can you say the word 'discharged' without lowering your voice? That word people once greeted with bouquets of flowers. Discharged! Go ahead, shout it out loud! Get well soon and be discharged early! Discharge Promotion League."

Incidentally, I could be mistaken but I think I have a rough idea of how the secretary compensated those five young shaven-headed fellows for handling the murder.

She stayed out of sight after that and didn't show up again until very late the next morning, close to noon. In one hand she was holding an envelope that contained a short letter of appointment for me, a bankbook, and a seal; her eyelids and nose were noticeably white, giving her a triumphant air, while the rest of her skin seemed muddy. Unless I imagined it, the slant of her hips had changed; they seemed to have fallen slightly. Even her way of walking seemed changed; now she walked with short, scuffling steps. My imagination whirled. If a woman not used to such activities had gone to bed with five young men one after the other, it was bound to affect the way she walked. And if my guess was right, this woman had an unlimited capacity for such compensation. A highly dangerous explosive was wandering around in our midst.

When I leave here after dark, it might be better to leave the notebook behind. The walls and ceiling are full of cracks, any one of which would make a good hiding place. I could put a map in with a letter, and mail it to some trustworthy person. . . .

(The girl woke up. I raised the back of the wheelchair for her. The change in her bodily shape is fairly evident now, but actually it seems to suit her, making her look rounder and younger.

When I held the urinal for her, she put her arms up around my neck. Her hair smelled like freshly boiled green peas. We ate a banana apiece, and drank some hot water from the thermos. My watch reads 2:46. That siren just now could have been the signal for three o'clock, though. The band had stopped for a while, but now they have struck up again. Sounds are reflected so diffusely in this underground passage that I can hardly make out what they are playing.)

Let me see, how far had I gotten? Oh yes, the horse had just put the last piece of raw fish and rice in his mouth.

"Yes, sir, she had her eye on you. Do you know what she told me? She said that you're the first man she ever met that she could imagine masturbating, without feeling sick."

"That's her problem, not mine."

The horse washed down the last bite with the rest of his beer, and slapped his abdomen with a loud noise like the crack of a wet cloth.

"Stimulating the abdominal muscles clears the head."

Next he took a waiting cassette down off the top of the cabinet, and inserted it in the deck of his large, very expensive-looking stereo set.

"Oh, cut it out. I'm not in the mood."

For an instant the horse looked puzzled; then he covered his mouth and emitted a long belch.

"Don't be silly. This is just a copy of the first part of that first tape. This is where that pill thief and your wife get together . . . assuming, of course, that that's what happened, I mean. . . . What do you say, why don't we play it back and try to figure everything out based on what we hear?"

He turned the switch on. We heard some kind of repeated noise in the background . . . footsteps, possibly rubber-soled sandals, coming closer . . . suddenly they became distinct, the background noise faded away. . . .

"What about this change in sound quality here? What's your opinion? When an automatic level control mechanism is operating, then if sounds close to the mike stop, distant sounds come in more clearly, don't they?"

"That's what it sounds like, all right."

"The mike picking up these sounds is in the pharmacy; not only that, it's in back of the very shelf where those pills were kept."

"What do you suppose was going on?"

"Probably he was substituting medicines. Anyway, he was in such close range of that supersensitive mike that it only comes through as noise."

"You think he heard footsteps, and stopped moving?"

"Right. That's why they keep coming closer."

The sound of footsteps, alone now, kept coming closer . . . they came to a halt . . . then, abruptly, a sharp, metallic click. . . .

"Is that the door?"

"From the pharmacy side it opens without a key, you know."

A short, dry, crashing sound . . . then a dull, heavy thud. . . .

"I wonder if she was attacked by the criminal?"

The horse stopped the tape and stroked his chin, stubbly with five o'clock shadow; the ends of his whiskers seemed to glisten.

"I hate to say it, but that does seem the likeliest possibility."

"But she would have screamed or something."

"Right. That bothered me, too. That's why I couldn't help thinking that they must have known each other after all."

"Then what about the sound right after that, like someone falling down; what do you make of that?"

"You could get a very similar sound by pushing over a bag of sodium bicarbonate or starch."

"I have another explanation just as good: My wife was running around then, looking for someone to lend her ten yen. When she realized there was someone in the pharmacy she felt relieved, and so when the criminal coolly opened the door and invited her inside, she . . ."

"Yes, hmm. Sensing no danger, she walks in as innocent as a lamb, and bingo, he takes her by surprise...."

The horse swung his hand down hard and slammed his fingers against the table's edge, frowning. A cup fell on the floor but did not break, saved evidently by the fine, thick carpet.

"Are there any leads on the pill thief?"

"What are you asking *me* for? You're the chief of security now."

"Stop playing games. You must know a thing or two more that you haven't told me yet."

"I have my own speculations. But speculations and facts aren't the same. About the only clear facts we have are on this tape right here."

"I'll bet the old chief of security was on to some other kind of information."

"Why?"

"Don't you think that's why he was killed—to keep him from spilling whatever it was he knew?"

"That figures. For her it would be killing two birds with one stone. It's not impossible."

"There must be an executive committee or something in charge of the anniversary eve party, isn't there?"

"I don't know the slightest thing about that."

"But it was brought up at the council meeting...."

"Somebody heard about it somewhere. Oh, sure, the day of the festival itself, I'll handle the greetings as usual. That's why I became a horse. But I don't know a thing about plans for the party the night before.... The council has a general policy of noninterference."

"But isn't it an authorized event? Somebody must have charge over the whole thing."

"Well, if anyone does, it must be you."

"Let me talk to the hospital director."

"Don't be unreasonable." The rain was coming down harder. The horse turned to face the dark window and stretched his back muscles, fingers linked behind his back. Framed by rain flickering like tongues of flame against the window pane, the expression on his reflected image began flickering, too.

"Who could ever understand the entire hospital? Of course, if it were possible I'd like to. Sometimes I want to know so much I start going crazy. But it takes courage even to say a thing like that. Much less to ask for the director . . . it's been years since anybody said that to me, or since I said it myself. Sometimes late at night, when I'm all alone, I get to thinking. I imagine the director somewhere inside the hospital worrying, imagining me not knowing where he is or what his name is or his specialty, or even whether or not he exists. . . ."

"I'll pay more attention and see if any news about the anniversary eve party comes in over the tapes."

"Good idea." He relaxed and turned around.

"Actually, you're not in a position to go snooping around too much, though. You're the head of security. You're supposed to know all about everything. Even if you don't, you've got to act as if you do and make people think so."

"That will work only so far. Whoever has my wife in custody, or captivity—I mean, whoever has hold of her—will surely see right through a pose like that."

"They may assume you've given silent consent."

"That's ridiculous."

The horse went and took a bottle of whiskey and two small glasses from a corner of the cupboard. He poured out two equal portions, lifted up his glass as if proposing a toast, and emptied its contents into his mouth as if he were swallowing a pill two centimeters around.

"Help yourself. You don't mind using your beer glass there for water, do you? Well, then, shall I have a look at that notebook?"

I figured there was no use haggling with him any more.

The horse had indeed supplied me with the promised information. As a result, at least it was plain that no particular mystery surrounded my wife's disappearance from the waiting room. My excitement at finding a clue, however, was surprisingly weak; instead, uneasiness filled me slowly but surely, like water seeping through a hole into a boat. Her encounter with the pill thief had to be a coincidence, and did nothing to answer the basic question of why an ambulance nobody had sent for had come in the first place. It was as though the question of my wife's whereabouts had slipped through a tiny crack of coincidence and dropped into the black depths of an unsuspected cavern.

"After two nights, this is as far as you've gotten. . . ." Skimming the final section of the notebook, the horse spoke sardonically. "You haven't even made it as far as the room yet. There must be something coming up that you're particularly anxious not to write about."

I returned the shot.

"There must be something coming up that you're particularly anxious to find out about."

The horse gave an unconcerned smile and poured himself another whiskey.

"Of course, you're going to work some more on this tonight, aren't you?"

"I don't know."

"Do it as a favor to me. Tomorrow's the party, and everything will be too hectic then."

"It's not true, is it?"

"What's not?"

"About giving the notebook to my wife . . ."

"Why?"

"It's all so unconvincing, every damn thing."

"There never would have been any problem if you'd only cooperated more. from the start." Suddenly his voice had tautened. His jaw moved slowly, as if he were chewing a whole pack of chewing gum at once, and the end of his nose turned white. That sort of excitement is catching. I felt that particles of electricity had been sprinkled across my chest and arms.

"Are you kidding? I've cooperated a hell of a lot more than I wish I had!"

"Come on, please? If it's too much trouble to write it all down, you can just tell me about it."

"About what?"

"You know what it is I want to know, don't you?"

"No; what? How big around my cock is?"

Suddenly the horse grabbed the whiskey bottle by its neck

and slammed it down on the table. He must have hurt his fingers before, and decided to use the bottle this time. For some reason the bottle didn't break, but a U-shaped crack appeared in the marble tabletop. I pressed it together, and it disappeared.

"These days you can get pretty strong porcelain adhesive, even at gas stations."

"You can't pretend you don't know." Heaving his shoulders slightly as he breathed, the horse ground his teeth. "I'm talking about the patient in room eight. It was the day your predecessor's lower half safely recovered its functioning and its nerves were successfully connected to mine. I had a meeting and dinner with some fellows from the artificial-organs and neural-engineering departments, who had done everything they could to be of help; it dragged on so late that by the time I got to room eight on my rounds it was after nine o'clock. The bed was empty. The very day that I was reborn as a horse, mind you. She'd been waiting for it, too. Somebody must have taken her out."

"Are you saying that I'm the one?"

"Of course, the prime suspect is your predecessor. He was her father, and unlike a good patient, he wasn't happy about our relationship. But you can't suspect someone who's been reduced to just his lower half. Besides, he has an alibi. He spent most of that day tied to the ends of my motor nerves with silicon-covered platinum wires."

"What do you mean, your 'relationship'? She's only thirteen years old. That little girl . . ."

"There's something fishy about the way you talk about her."

"Well, if you suspected me, why didn't you come out and say so from the start? It's ridiculous. Making me waste all this time churning out a report on myself. . . ."

"Because I couldn't quite believe it."

"I'm afraid I'd better be going."

"No, you don't. There isn't the slightest room for doubt any more that you are the guilty one."

"Have you got proof?"

"You bet I do." The horse flung the notebook down on

the table, but not as hard as he might have. "Take a look. It's all right in there."

"You're putting me on."

"In both notebooks you always went out of your way to mention just where you were doing the writing. A cheap trick, I must say. Today when I phoned to say I was coming for you, you happened to be in your room, so you had to stay put. But yesterday and the day before you were hardly ever in. Even at night, you were always out somewhere. My secretary and I chased around after you, so don't try to make up any excuses."

"Couldn't you keep up with me?"

"I never saw anybody run so fast."

"Shall I order you a pair of jump shoes, too?"

"Look, I give up. Come on, she has to have medical attention. It's been three days already."

"No, it hasn't. Just two full days."

"She has a disease called osteolysis. It's a nasty thing; the bones dissolve and turn to liquid. And if treatment isn't kept up, the effect of gravity sets off axial shrinkage. If she starts turning into horrible shapes, it will be all your fault. Please, for crying out loud. This way, I went to all the trouble of becoming a horse for nothing."

"What a sob story; it's not like you."

"In this morning's test my extra penis performed beautifully. I wish you could have seen it. It's seven centimeters around and nineteen long, you know. The nurses were all breathless with admiration."

"Well, you won't have any lack of partners, will you, what with your wife, your secretary, and now the nurses."

"Don't talk dirty. You don't understand. You don't know how precious that girl is to me. . . ."

"But all you did was watch while she masturbated, isn't that so?"

"Listen, I'm not talking about cocks and cunts. If it was just masturbation, I could see that at any strip show. This is a problem of philosophy. 'A good doctor makes a good patient.' Don't you see?"

"It seemed to me the only problem was the cock."

"Every doctor eventually goes through a kind of philosophical stricture." He began talking faster, like a spider spinning out its web; I couldn't help thinking, however, that there was a discrepancy between what he said and what he was thinking. "When a person is hurt the important thing isn't sympathy for the pain, but somebody to stop the bleeding, disinfect the wound, and sew it up. You have to treat the injured person not like a human being with a wound, but like a *human wound*. For a doctor who's used to such relationships, nothing is more maddening than a patient who acts like a goddam human being. To keep from arousing his doctor's anger, the patient tries to stop being human. The doctor becomes more and more alone, his nerves go on edge, and he drifts farther and farther from humanity. I guess you could even say a prejudice against patients is one requirement for a great doctor.

"Paradoxically, though, the loneliness of doctors is itself the most human thing there is. Only man has turned away from the law of survival of the fittest, taken up the weak and ailing, and guaranteed their right to survival. So heroes perish, but the weak live on. One measure of a civilization, in fact, is the percentage of misfits in its society. There's even a political scientist (anonymous) who claims that our modern age is an age 'of the patient, by the patient, and for the patient.' So people shouldn't go around complaining that this is a sick age. In a way, the doctor's loneliness is the patient's right. But if the doctor wants to escape his loneliness, then all he can do is become a patient and take on dual qualifications. That's been my attitude all along. That's why I never worried about being impotent. It's really true. Being impotent made me that much closer to the patients, so it was actually kind of comforting."

"What do you mean? You yourself told me once that the longer a patient stays around, the more likely his sexual appetite is to increase."

"I was just getting to that. As the number of buggings has gone up, it's become an inescapable fact. There doesn't seem to be any impotence among real patients. It doesn't count as a sickness. But why is that? It may have something to do with the structure of patients' society. In prisons and army barracks, telling dirty stories is the key to making friends. In behind-the-scenes business dealings, it's usually effective to provide free sex. Married couples who are tired of each other can in many cases get through the dangerous period by charging an entrance fee to the bedroom. All of these are ways of using sex to reconstruct personal relationships. Of course, the patients' society is not the same as a prison or an army barracks. There's no need to avoid the eyes of others, and there isn't the crisis of a breakdown in personal relationships. But somewhere in the structure of their society must be hidden the secret of how to lighten the central burden of personal relationships.

"What is a patient? What constitutes the essence of being a patient? Suddenly it hit me. That girl, anyway, helps me to forget my impotence. She unlocks the door to my doctor's cage, and beckons me into the patients' territory. It could only be because she possesses the spirit of perfect patientness. A spirit so generous that she can share it with me. I want to find a way inside her mind. I want to at least try to be like her in spirit. . . ."

"Sorry, but there isn't the slightest resemblance."

"The ideal patient . . . the patient among patients . . . the forever incurable patient . . . days spent sleeping curled up with death . . . a parasitic vine grown larger than its host . . . deformity personified . . . a monster . . . and finally, a 'horseman.'"

"But don't you realize—that extra cock you have belonged to that girl's father!"

"Ah, but intercourse isn't something you do with your genitals, it's something you do with your personal relations center."

"Whatever that's supposed to mean. A pretty self-serving argument, if you ask me."

"Of course, the genitals do function to arouse desire. An American doctor named Brash or something like that has discovered that the sensation caused by friction on the mucous membranes of the genitals is very like the sensation of itching. Itchiness occurs in a physiological system when some type of foreign matter starts to build up in the immediate environment, in order to diffuse that foreign matter through mechanical friction (in other words, scratching). First the sense organs in the skin, under stimulus from the foreign matter, create a substance in the environment called ATC (if I'm remembering this right), thereby sending a signal to the brain, which registers the sensation of itchiness. That sensation triggers the urge to scratch. Again, in the case of sexual impulses, some substance like ATC builds up in the mucous membrane of the genitals. But in this case the sensation is not as well defined as 'itchiness'; it's somewhat vaguer, more like a burning or a dull ache. So conditions imposed by the brain take on great significance: as long as conditions for restraint are not removed, then neither the burning sensation nor the dull ache can be translated into the sexual act itself. In other words, as long as the personal relations center, which plays the part of lookout, doesn't pull the starter switch, then it's impossible to get in the proper frame of mind."

"If you want it that bad, why not just smash down the lookout post?"

"Listen here . . . you took that girl away from me, but I haven't taken anything away from you, don't forget."

"It's all the same thing. The hospital did."

"But for all we know, your wife may have applied."

"Applied for what?"

"To be in the pre-festival orgasm contest. Yes, that would explain everything. They were advertising for contestants pretty widely, and she must have had it all worked out with the pill thief beforehand. Still, it took some thinking to use an ambulance like that. Some hospital insider must have helped her out."

"Sorry, but both of us are in the pink of health. There's no way she could have had any contact with the hospital."

"The boundary between the hospital and the outside world isn't as firm as you think it is. Hmm, if your wife did apply voluntarily, then even if we do track down her hiding place, it's not going to be easy after that."

"What about the girl from room eight? If she ran away from that room of her own free will, then even if you find out *her* hiding place, it won't be easy after that."

"Listen here: I don't know where your wife is."

"You listen here: I don't have any idea where that girl is, either."

The horse and I were both deeply hurt. He had been standing all this time, while I sat in a chair; we glared at each other, making no attempt to hide our quickened breathing. I was first to turn my eyes away. I did so only because my contact lens was about to slip out of place; it had no other meaning.

"What are you just standing there like that for? You cut off the view."

The horse loosened his belt, unzipped his fly, and let his trousers fall down around his knees; then he rolled up his shirt. A black synthetic-rubber corset about five millimeters thick totally encased his middle, from just under his rib cage to midway down his thighs. Its surface was crisscrossed with variegated electrical wires, with a gold-plated electrode at every point where they crossed. At his crotch was an opening like a vertical letter slot, where his penis hung down limply like moldy Chinese food, framed by pubic hair like a metal scrub brush.

"See? I haven't got much choice."

"All right, you've made your point, so pull up your pants, please."

When he wound a microcomputer belt under the corset and fastened on his auxiliary lower half, complete with miniature life-sustaining equipment (portable), a transfer of nerve sensations took place. Since he was unable to take the corset off unassisted, however, he had to spend all his time either standing up or lying down, except for once every three days or so, when he had the thing cleaned at the artificial organs department. If I ever felt generous enough to forgive him, which didn't seem likely, I thought it would be nice to design a chair for him so that he could relax while standing up.

Pulling up his trousers, he said, "Okay, if you're that positive, then how about taking a lie detector test like you promised?"

"Fine with me."

In point of fact, I was worried about the girl from room eight, and wanted to get out of there as fast as I could. I had left her alone almost five hours, waiting for me in that underground passage. I had made sure she had plenty of drinking water and food, but she was probably bored and feeling lost and alone above all. Besides, with this rain I was afraid that water might start to seep in.

I knew, though, that there were bound to be several of the secretary's shaven-headed henchmen lurking in shadows around the building, waiting for me to leave. I wasn't too sure of the geography around there, and had no confidence that I would be able to shake them off my tail. Fortunately, the horse's wife, who was the lie detector specialist, lived in quarters by the Psycholinguistics Center. Since the machine was in the center, of course the test would be held there. The center was in a square white building that lay east of the main grounds, across the street from the hospital cemetery. In order to shut out all noise and light from the outside, it had no windows, and was designed to be entered and left from below ground. From there I would be able to make use of the cemetery layout to shake off any tail they cared to put on me.

Of course, I wasn't really serious about taking the test. I intended to think of some appropriate excuse to get rid of the horse, and then win over his wife and persuade her to cancel or postpone it.

My image of the assistant director's wife had been quite mistaken. After all, I had thought, she was intelligent enough to have risen straight from plain patient-typist to full-fledged researcher on the strength of a single article, entitled "The Logic of Lying: Adapting Toward Structure Through Ritualization." And knowing that she had been self-centered enough to leave her husband on grounds of impotence, I couldn't help picturing someone like a mechanical drawing in drag.

When I actually met her, I was taken completely by surprise. Except for a certain shrewd and determined quality in her nose and upper lip, her subcutaneous fat was distributed across her body in perfect proportion. Her eyes were sad and heavy as ripe grapes; her voice was soft and breathy, and the collar of her uniform was crisp even in midafternoon.

I changed my mind and decided to take the test after all. I think now I must have been gasping for a sensation of normalcy, like someone gulping for air underwater. It wasn't only a reaction to the horse's abnormality, and to all the strange happenings around there; my confidence in the reliability of my own internal mirror had begun to waver.

When she came to the dangerous questions, all I had to do was refuse to answer.

She received me as cordially as I had hoped. She even told me frankly all about her reasons for separating from her husband. The day they were married they had made a bizarre agreement to confirm all their conversations with each other using the lie detector. Their decision had not been based on jealousy or suspicion; it had been a free choice, meant actually as a positive, naïve confirmation of their love. Not to blame but to forgive, they had sought to eliminate the artifice of lies.

Results had undermined all their expectations, producing just the opposite effect from that intended. Day after day the vital tension between them had weakened until in the end nothing was left but an empty space like unexposed film.

"It wasn't that anything had changed especially. It was just like a light bulb with no electric current. I guess lie detectors have a freezing effect. And if truth is the front, then lies are the back; you end up thinking of everything in terms of front and back."

"Sounds pretty dismal."

"Even computers think of everything in binary terms. Yes or no. That might work if there were never any contradiction between feelings and reason. But take away that contradiction from people and what do you think would be left? If there were nothing but facts, no lies or truth . . ."

"Things would certainly be logical."

"That was what I hated more than anything else about myself."

After they had ceased to have dialogue, the magnetism

between them had gone, too. Nothing had been left to hold them together, and nothing to push them apart; there had been only their dried-out hearts, like empty insect shells. The assistant director had become chronically impotent, and the head of the Psycholinguistics Center had prescribed a trial separation for their own good.

"So your article on 'The Logic of Lying' was based on your own experiences?"

"Have you read it?"

"I'm sure it's way over my head. . . ."

"Well, for example, there are social lies, such as calling the announcement that two people are about to begin sexual relations a 'wedding,' or calling the period of temporary seclusion when they devote themselves to sex a 'honeymoon.' That does away with the sense of indecency, doesn't it? When the sex act is made a ritual, then the body's personal relations center can relax and issue its own permit."

"That's the second time today I've heard that term 'personal relations center.'"

"Three times is bad for the heart." She laughed and finished adjusting the machine. "May I begin?"

"Go right ahead."

She began a long succession of flat, colorless questions. Do you like dogs? . . . Is it morning now? . . . Is it raining? . . . Have you ever eaten a tomato? . . . Do you brush your teeth before you wash your face? . . . Did you dream in color last night? . . .

Then all at once she hit me with a totally unexpected question.

"Do you want to sleep with me?" When I was unable to answer, she looked at the graph lines on the roll of paper and smiled, biting her lower lip with white teeth. "There, you told a lie."

"But I didn't say anything yet."

"Whatever you say will be a lie."

"That's not fair."

"Adultery is the personal relations center's number one enemy."

"All right, ask me again."

"Do you want to sleep with me?"

"Yes."

"That's funny. . . ."

"It came out true, right?"

"Your personal relations center must not be working. . . . I'll bet the lie detector test is serving the purpose of ritualization."

"How about getting on with the last question?"

But instead she turned off the machine and started to remove the electrodes from my body.

"You never meant to answer anyway, did you?"

Her throat tightened as if she were talking to someone else in the distance. If she hadn't cut off the questioning for my sake, but as a kind of declaration aimed at the assistant director, then perhaps she was trying to tell him that now that he had become a horse and recovered from his impotence, he should come back to her. When I tried to picture the horse having intercourse with his extra penis, it seemed more obscene, somehow, to imagine him doing it with her than with anyone else. But in my mind the word "obscene" seemed to have acquired positive connotations, such as "mellow" or "ripe."

"Do you still want to sleep with me?"

For some reason I was unable to answer. Perhaps without the electrodes, the ritual had ended. She said shyly that she would like to take my picture, and snapped four or five Polaroid shots of me wearing nothing but a pair of shorts, from several different angles. It made me slightly sad to imagine her staring at the photographs alone at night. It seemed so unfair that such a rich body should be so lonely. And yet in a way it seemed to suit her so well.

Regretfully I saw her back to her apartment, and then went out to the street by the cemetery. In the dim light of the few streetlights, the wet, straight paved road was as black as water in a stagnant canal. Nothing could have been blacker; even a black kitten crossing the road would have stood out against it. I crossed leisurely over to the cemetery side, cleared a shoulder-high cement-block wall, and checked back through the dense cherry tree branches. Just as I had expected, about three seconds later five human figures crossed the road behind me. Were they the same ones who did in my predecessor, or was the secretary just partial to groups of five?

For a while I walked along attracting my pursuers' attention by kicking stones and rattling branches. Then suddenly I started to run. Not along the road, though; using obstacle-course racing technique, I vaulted over gravestones, running in a beeline, ignoring the road. Luckily, in that weather there was no danger of colliding with couples engaged in secret rendez-vous. The rain had stopped and the half moon, racing through rifts in the clouds, lit up the wet gravestone heads for me. The gravestones were a good height for jump shoes, but with ordi-nary sporting shoes you would have to climb laboriously up on each one and then jump down again. That alone would produce a time gap. Besides, even though the stones were laid out in a strict checkerboard pattern, each one faced in a slightly differ-ent direction; the road followed the gravestones, so it wound as intricately as an arabesque design. Whoever had designed the place must have been strongly opposed to any communication among the dead. Even for the living, it was difficult to decide after clearing one stone which grave lay in a straight line from there. As the distance between me and my pursuers gradually increased, they would begin to lose their sense of direction, and scatter; chasing after one another, they would eventually lose sight of me.

I regulated my breathing, put bounce in my knees, and ran on quickly and smoothly. Before long the five sets of foot-steps behind me were bound to falter, mix in confusion, and then recede in the distance. But as it turned out, equally smooth footwork followed me closely wherever I went, like a second shadow. I thought I must be imagining things, and tried speed-ing up. The footsteps behind me did likewise. I tried changing direction. Like a school of killifish, in an instant they shifted direction with me. Somehow they must have got hold of jump shoes of their own. Maybe one of the guys from the company had campaigned here successfully. I couldn't let anyone get away with stealing a march on me like that. Or had these fellows just gone and ordered them themselves? I wished they had done it through me, since I was in sales. I had a right to a fixed commission on every sale, and it affected my sales record, too.

Little by little I started running out of breath. They seemed to have figured me out; the five of them were spread out in a grid, like dogs hunting down a rabbit. Every time I changed direction, a new pursuer would take over. But since I was the only one being chased, there was a definite limit as to how long it could go on. They did not seem bent on trying to catch me, though; their strategy seemed to be to continue this game of hide-and-seek until my patience gave out and I ran back to the hideout. What if I never went back; what would the girl from room eight do? In despair at my betrayal, and in terror of rats, she might burst into tears and scream for help with all her might. That would play into their hands, too, I was cornered.

Hold on, though—wasn't I the chief of security, with three black stripes to prove it? That made me their direct superior whether they liked it or not. I had no idea what the assistant director's secretary might have told them, but it could do no harm to try a test of my own authority. If it failed I would at least be no worse off.

I jumped up on a gravestone (there was a noise like a tiny bell rolling), spun around, and yelled out a command at the top of my lungs.

"Everyone stop! Don't move!"

There was no need to repeat it. My timing and tone must have been exactly right. My pursuers became unmoving shadows in the darkness, then disappeared. Insects began to sing. It was a new experience for me, and I suspect for them, too. If my predecessor had only known how to give commands he might not have been murdered so helplessly.

I ran through the darkness alongside the infirmary until I came to the old, weed-covered hospital site. I listened awhile to the voices of the insects, making sure I hadn't been followed, then crawled through a half-flooded sewer pipe, emerging through a toilet hole. I groped my way down a hall that was half buried in rubble from crumbling walls, feeling my way ahead; finally I came to the steel pipe I had been watching for (it stuck out from the ceiling, and for some reason, when I put my ear up to it I could hear noises of railway construction), and switched on my flashlight.

Slipping through narrow spaces in the rubble, after a time I emerged into a fairly secure concrete hallway. Beyond the wooden door at the end of the hall was our hideout. I thought I heard a moan of pain, and abandoning caution, I began to sprint. When the sound of my footsteps did not evoke the reaction I had expected, I became even more concerned. I burst through the door just as the girl was having an orgasm. Pretending not to notice, I bent down and gave her a strong hug, ignoring the wrist busily at work between her thighs. I could not be sure, but it seemed that the resiliency of her body had subtly changed. Had the liquefaction of her bones progressed even further? Her wrist stopped moving, and she threw her arms around me with all her strength. She began to sob, then to tremble with uncontrollable violence.

I am just back from another survey of the anniversary-eve party site, from the top of the hill on the old hospital grounds. A few more people had gathered than before, but the place was still quiet. I could tell that something was about to happen, though, from the way the owners of concession stands by the park were bustling around lighting portable burners and preparing to open for business.

I made a simple meal out of a curry roll and some apple juice. To keep the girl from shrinking any more, I lowered the back of her wheelchair until it was horizontal, and began to massage her spine; I stopped in three minutes when she started to show signs of arousal. Thanks to an outside antenna I attached to the ventilator, radio reception is much better now. Listening through earphones, she is beginning to nod sleepily.

I may as well go on writing awhile longer.

I cannot explain to my own satisfaction, let alone defend,

the inherent contradiction in my hiding out here like this with the girl from room eight while ostensibly searching for my wife. Doubtless I am not the only one who finds it difficult to accept. Any normal human being would sneer at such deceit.

But it was only last night that I learned about the possibility of contact between my wife and the pill thief. It seems to me that no allowance can be made for the horse's breach of faith in pretending to know nothing until then. The only way I can get back at him for that is by not returning the girl. Early this morning I telephoned security headquarters and ordered them to gather data on the pill thief on a top-priority basis. Yes, "ordered"; last night's experience taught me the effectiveness of an order. Since then I have been going outside every two hours to listen to the reports. Unfortunately, as of this moment not a single one has given me any cause for hope.

Or could it be that the secretary is interfering? The more I think about it, the likelier it seems that she had my predecessor killed not so much to provide the assistant director with a substitute for the emergency doctor as to stop the chief from disclosing something he knew about the pill thief. If she was determined to get me too, then I would have to watch my step. If it came to a question of letting me escape alive or taking me dead, she would probably choose the latter.

Whenever I am out, I take the opportunity to do a little snooping around myself. It could be the white security supervisor's uniform with its three black stripes, but so far not one person has refused to cooperate. Doctors, nurses, other employees, patients, all of them have come volunteering information of their own accord. The only trouble is that everything they tell me is a transparent fabrication. Or if not an out-and-out lie, then it is an analysis of thieves in general, or a speculation on possible new crimes using the pills. Thus there is no way to act on the reports, much as I wish I could. To give them all the benefit of the doubt, probably they are simply unwilling to plead ignorance in the face of a direct command of the chief of security. The gang of pill thieves seems to be operating in strict secrecy.

No matter how secretly they may carry on their activities, though, it's only a matter of time now. Once the curtain rises on the anniversary eve party, they won't be able to stay under cover like this any more. Since the whole point of it all has been preparation for a party stunt, they will be forced to show themselves then. Every year at five o'clock the assistant director cuts the customary tape, and the drumbeats announce the official opening. In another hour or two it will automatically come to a showdown. Even now, as I sit waiting, second by second I am closing in on them. No one can halt the advance of time.

From the time I was a boy, though, I was never very fond of festivals. They always fill me with an ominous foreboding. I am too conscious of the devils at another festival beyond the one visible, staring curiously my way.

(I drink down a bottle of tonic and light my fourth cigarette of the day. I take out my contact lenses and massage my eyes for a while. My tear glands make squeaky little noises like tree frogs. The girl is breathing softly in her sleep. Sleep is all very well, but I have a feeling she's overdoing it a bit. I hope it isn't a sign that her condition is getting worse. . . .)

Let me see. It was the morning after I was appointed chief of security. I didn't want to be labeled an accessory to the crime for having watched the murder of the former chief in silence, so I intended at least to let the assistant director know that I had been an eyewitness, and try to find out where the responsibility lay. The assistant director never showed his face around the main building, however, so I set out for the cartilage surgery ward myself.

Eight in the morning is the busiest, most active hour on a ward. Children having blood drawn scream and wail; white-uniformed nurses sweep from room to room bearing thermometers; patients holding urine bottles in their hands wander down the halls; practical nurses argue with patients over whether the windows should be open or closed; and young male patients have their stiffened penises batted by the fingertips of female doctors.

I went directly to the third floor and tried knocking on the director's door; there was no answer, even though the IN sign was hanging up. I turned the handle, and the door opened. The emergency doctor was nowhere in sight, but there were the two beds that I had seen that first day through the peephole in the ceiling of room eight, and a confused melee of electrical gadgets and equipment. Over by the wall was an office desk. It struck me that the lower wall paneling behind it seemed slightly loose. That would be the way through to the opening in room eight. I closed the door and latched it, then crawled under the desk and explored the paneling. It was an amateurish job, with a wire ring fastened in one corner. When I pulled on the ring a section of paneling just the width of the desk came out in my hand. From that side it was easy to remove, but it might have been more difficult from the other side.

Light was shining from within. Head down, I crawled slowly inside. Rusty-smelling particles of dust entered my nostrils; my chest hurt as if it would burst, but I suppressed the desire to sneeze. To keep from making noise, I groped my way down the ladder hand over hand, one rung at a time, finally hanging upside down with my knees spread apart, braced for support against the walls. Through a crack in the curtain I could just make out the lower half of the room. The girl was naked. Hips thrust out, knees open, she was rubbing her slender hands on her small kneecaps, bobbing her head up and down and panting like a long-distance runner. At her feet was the assistant director, one hand draped across her thigh, the other rubbing his own crotch on top of his trousers. He seemed to be saying something, but I couldn't catch what it was. Anyway, the scene was a bit much for eight o'clock in the morning.

Hurriedly I crawled back up out of the hole, and stamped noisily around by the paneling. That way, thinking that someone was already in the upstairs room, the assistant director would be unable to use the secret passageway and would be forced to go around from the outside to see who it was. But since I had latched the door from the inside, he wouldn't be able to get in. It would take him twenty or thirty minutes before he gave up and went to call for help.

Everything went just as I had planned. I heard the door of room eight open and shut, waited a moment or two, and then climbed down feet first. When the girl saw me, somehow she didn't seem very surprised. I smiled at her, and she sucked on a finger and smiled back shyly.

"Let's hurry. Where's your suitcase?"

"I haven't got one."

"You need some clothes."

"Haven't got any of those either."

She lifted her rolled-up pajamas in the air, holding them in her toes. Her legs were so long, slender, and lithe that it was hard to believe she had a bone disease.

"Okay then, put those on."

Still lying down, she obediently put her arms through the pajama sleeves. In the meantime, I checked her bedside stand. Two bananas, a papaya cut in half, a hair dryer with brush, two ball point pens, two girls' magazines, some unfinished lace, and a red leather purse with a bell attached. The clasp on the purse was broken, and the contents fell out on the floor: 6,300 yen in cash, a blood-type badge, a patient's registration form, a gold fox three millimeters big, and an eighteen-carat ring with a small stone like a hardened drop of blood. I spread out a towel, laid her washbowl on it, packed everything inside, and tied it up loosely by the four corners. That way I would be able to sling it across my shoulder and have both arms free for the girl.

"Can you walk?"

She had just got her pajama bottoms on, and was sitting on the edge of the bed. Cocking her head to one side, she braced herself with both arms and slid slowly off the bed. She managed to stand up, but immediately stuck out her arms and started to fall. I held out an arm to her, and she grabbed it tightly and regained her balance, smiling so happily that her two front teeth shone. Leaning on my arm, she took a step forward, tongue thrust out between her teeth. Lines of dirt were caked on her ear lobe.

"It's so high. . . ."

"What is?"

"It's like looking out of a two-story window."

"You mean you've never stood up and walked by yourself before?"

"I used to be fatter."

"This is impossible. I'll have to carry you."

"When my body stretches out too suddenly, the nerves are pulled and I get tired real easy."

We didn't have much time. If there was another way into the director's room on the third floor, any minute now he would notice the missing plywood, and see through the whole scheme.

"Is the intercom switch on or off?"

"Off."

Hanging the bundle around my neck so that it lay down across my chest, I picked the girl up on my back and carried her out into the hall. I had expected to draw stares, but evidently in a hospital strange sights are less conspicuous, not more. No one even gave us a second glance. The fact that it was eight in the morning must have been in our favor, too.

Still, I had an idea that the elevator might be risky. She was stuck on my back as closely as crude rubber; I could hardly feel her weight. I sprinted down the stairs and was about to dash through the waiting room toward the exit when I pulled up short. My instincts had been right. Among the people standing waiting for the elevator was the assistant director's secretary. No doubt she was after me. They were all looking up impatiently at the dial. The elevator seemed to be stuck somewhere, perhaps unloading freight. The heel of the secretary's sandal tapped out a restless staccato against the floor, moving gradually faster and faster. What if she gave up waiting and decided to take the stairs? After all, she was the one who had masterminded that plot to kill the father of the little girl on my back. In such emergencies, the eyes automatically search out a way of escape. High piles of wooden crates had kept me from noticing before, but now I saw that the stairs went on down behind the crates and below ground.

Somehow I squeezed behind the piles of crates. Stealthily I

crept to the bottom of the stairs and came out into a dark
corridor, lit only by the little light that straggled down from
between the crates. There was a cold draft that smelled like the
musty air under old cellar floorboards.

"Where are we going?"

"Let's see, where shall we go?"

I could hardly say that we were on our way to get lost. I
decided to start out walking.

"When you get tired of walking, let's stop and eat a banana."

"I just started."

The corridor angled left and was darker than ever. As my
eyes adjusted to the darkness, however, I discovered that there
was just enough light to see where I was going. The corridor
went on and on. Mentally reviewing the design of the building,
I was puzzled. We had to have left the building grounds behind
some time ago. There were no turnoffs, and no rooms on either
side. Perhaps it was not an ordinary corridor, then, but an
underground passage leading to some other building.

"Let's go back."

"No."

"But you forgot my urinal."

"I'll buy you another one real soon."

"Where are we going?"

"Where would you like to go?"

"Someplace brighter."

"It won't be long now."

I was getting tired. I thought we had come pretty far, but I
wasn't sure. Since I was walking slowly, we might not have
covered much distance yet.

"Where do you live?"

"I used to live in ward three . . . before Mother turned into
a quilt."

"Before she turned into a what?"

"A quilt. You know, you put it over you when you go to
sleep, and it's got cotton inside."

"How did she do that?"

The girl trembled suddenly and told me that she was in

pain, speaking in a voice so low that I could barely hear. It must not have been wise to keep her in one position for such a long time. Hurriedly I put her down on the floor, sat myself against the wall, and set her on my lap with my arm around her. She leaned against me limply, her cheek against the back of my hand where it lay on her shoulder. It didn't seem to be anything serious. The corridor wall was made of rough concrete, and it dug into my back. The floor was damp; I felt uncomfortable. But neither did I feel like getting up and walking on again right away. It wouldn't do to go back, and yet there was no point in going ahead, either. It was as though we had got lost on our way to get lost.

"Is the pain better?"

"Uh-huh."

"How did your mother turn into a quilt?"

"Did you ever hear of watafuki disease?"

"No."

"It's when cotton starts to come out of the pores in your skin."

"You don't mean real cotton. It must be some kind of fat or something."

"No, cotton. They tested it in the lab and everything."

"Huh. That's funny."

"At first it was here, on the back of her hand. . . ."

She took my hand, the one her cheek had been leaning against, and traced on it with a fingertip. "It happened when I was real little, but I still remember. It was like a scary dream; you could pull it out piece by piece. No matter how much you pulled, there was always more. . . . Pretty soon there were big holes in the skin on her hands, and you could see the bones. She said it didn't hurt, but Daddy was worried and he put some Mercurochrome on it. But since it was just cotton, the Mercurochrome only soaked in right away and didn't do any good. He put on so much, he ended up using a whole bottle. Her hands looked like red cotton gloves. When you held them up to the light you could see the bones perfectly. The next day she went in the hospital, but it was already too late. They said she was full of cotton everywhere, in her neck, her bottom, her ears, even inside her breasts. The doctor said it was best to get rid of it fast before it spread any more, so Daddy and I picked cotton every day. Her hands and feet looked like the bones had on big baggy gloves and socks; it was awful creepy. Six months after she went in the hospital, the cotton went to her heart, and she died. That was terrible. We had picked enough cotton altogether to fill three kerosene-stove crates, so we had a quilt made out of it. I wanted to keep it, but my stupid Daddy said that was too morbid, and went and gave it to a museum. I'll bet he wanted to get an award or something. It's still there in the museum, but just the same, it's really my quilt."

As soon as she finished talking her breathing changed; she fell fast asleep. To keep from disturbing her, I stayed motionless, patiently enduring the hardness of the wall and the wetness of the floor.

(I just came back from my sixth phone call to security headquarters. There was still nothing on the pill thief. I was taken aback when the florist's son urged me in a sickeningly sweet voice to hurry back because the assistant director and his secretary were worried about me. Or was he trying to tell me ironically that they had tracked down our hideout long ago?

On the way back, wary of being followed, I took a slightly different route. I went underground from the bottom of a pond by the museum (now dried up), near cages where animals were once kept. That way is many times farther than the underground passageway, and if I weren't careful it would be easy to get lost. Exactly for that reason, it is also quite safe. I mean to take the same route when I go to the anniversary eve party, so this was also a little reconnaissance trip for that purpose. Along the way I came upon one place where a brick wall had collapsed, blocking the passage. I cleared the rubble to one side, making just enough space for the wheelchair to get by.

The museum garden overlooks the party grounds from behind. There still wasn't much sign of the proper atmosphere as far as I could tell, except for that rock band sullenly practicing in front of the fountain across the street in the park, while their leader yelled frantically at them and a few patients looked idly on. Maybe the party isn't as big an event as it's built up to be after all. I met an elderly couple dragging a concession stand down the road in front of the park, from the direction of the wards. Both of them were patients, one suffering from chronic gastritis and the other from pituitary cachexia (Simmonds' disease); with rapt, dreamy expressions, they told me, speaking in the past tense, about all the enthusiasm and excitement the party used to generate every year.

It's almost four now. Have I been bluffing all this time just for a legendary illusion? That's why you can't trust festivals.)

I must have slept, too. The girl's voice woke me up.

"What's that noise?"

"Probably a bug."

"Is it true that cemeteries have bugs that eat the dead bodies?"

"Nowadays everybody is cremated."

"That's true."

I hurt all over. My crossed legs were pressing hard into my calves. I shifted my position. The girl screamed, then said apologetically in a surprisingly mature voice, "My bones are melting little by little, like gelatin. When I change my position the effect of gravity changes, too, so the flow of my bones changes and the nerves get pulled around. That's why it hurts."

"What position is most comfortable for you?"

"It doesn't make any difference. I can get used to any position right away. . . ."

Drops fell on my wrist where I was supporting her head. I was unable to tell if they were tears or drops of drool. I ran my free hand down along the curve of her spine. It was quite a bit different from the normal curvature. I couldn't tell what position she was in. Had her entire skeletal structure changed to adapt to the contour of my crossed legs?

"Try to bear it, okay?"

Alarmed, I lowered her off my knees and leaned her gently against the wall, as carefully as if she were a disjointed doll. She seemed pretty misshapen. Maybe it was only that sensations were exaggerated in the darkness.

"I shrank a lot."

"No, you didn't."

My luminous watch dial was hard to make out. The two hands were overlapping; the time seemed to be somewhere between eight and nine. Eight forty-four, evidently. I thought I had slept a long time, but it must have been only a moment or two.

Slowly, like a lump of butter being squeezed in the hand, my sense of reality returned. No, it must be 8:44 *p.m.* It had been about eight-forty in the morning when I took the girl out of her room. It was impossible to believe that only four minutes had elapsed since then. It felt like at least half an hour. Had I slept for nearly twelve hours? The luminous paint on the watch was starting to fade, another indication that a considerable amount of time must have gone by. No wonder the child's body had become distorted. The pain in my own body sharpened. Tiny stones felt embedded in the flesh of my buttocks, and something sharp was digging into my ribs. She must be in even worse pain.

"How long do you think we were asleep?"

"I don't know, but I'm sick of it."

"I hardly slept all day yesterday."

"I saved you half a banana."

"Shall I help you go to the bathroom?"

"I already did, by myself."

I tried to stand up, and fell over. My left leg was so fast asleep that I could hardly tell it was there. Groping in the dark, I spread out the girl's towel, smoothed my uniform jacket out on top of it, then added my pants and shirt. I picked up the girl and laid her down on top of the pile. At least the floor was level there; that was one good thing.

"Wait here, all right? I'll be right back."

"I want to go home."

"How can you? You just ran away."

"I don't want to run away."

"I'm going to go find you a wheelchair, okay?"

"I want to take a bath."

"I'll give you a bath later. Is there anything else you want? I'll try not to forget the urinal, either. And it's dark, so we'll need a flashlight."

"If I'm not in bed I'll start to turn all funny shapes."

"I'll get you a quilt, then."

"What one?"

"Something to go with the wheelchair. What's your favorite color?"

"My mother's quilt . . ."

"The one in the museum, you mean? It must be all moldy."

"Then let's go back."

"Okay, okay, I'll get your mother's quilt."

"I don't care. I'm scared."

"Here, feel these biceps. When I was in school I used to be a boxing champion."

The back of her hand was cold and dry, but her palm was hot and moist. She seemed awfully tense. I stroked her cheek, then ran my fingers through her hair once or twice.

"There's lice here."

"I'll come right back. . . ."

One hand on the wall, one arm groping ahead like a feeler in the darkness, I ran off, dressed in nothing but my shorts.

It is not sour grapes; I actually do think that in the end those haphazard actions of mine were for the best. If I hadn't made what appeared to be the stupid blunder of going to sleep for nearly twelve hours, then everything would have been completely different.

That underground passageway was an old corridor between the old hospital building, now a weed-buried relic reduced to its foundations, and the cartilage surgery department; cartilage surgery was part of the old complex anyway. The passageway connected the cartilage surgery (formerly general surgery) basement with the third floor of the old main building, and had evidently once been in frequent use.

Afterward I found out that we had gone almost to the end

of that passageway. In less than ten meters or so I would have had to stop and choose between a flight of stairs leading up on the left, and another corridor going off to the right. Since we still had no wheelchair at that time, it probably would have made more sense to go up the stairs, where a faint light could be seen. At the top of the stairs the corridor turned right and ran into a rotting wooden door. As I looked through the key-hole of that door, blue sky would have been shining over lush summer grasses, for all the world as though promising safety. Had I pushed down the door and stepped outside, I would have been greeted with cries of laughter from overhead. We would have been trapped in a concrete box, with the owners of the laughter looking down on us from the old building's clock tower, one of my pursuers' best observation points.

But after twelve hours went by, my pursuers had begun to relax their lookout. The wards had been searched so care-fully in every nook and cranny that by then they were practi-cally a safety zone. I managed to find a Swedish wheelchair of the latest model, as well as everything else we needed, from three kinds of flashlights (large, medium, and small) and a hi-fi FM radio to a big thermos bottle.

The girl was delighted with the wheelchair. Its big, silver-chrome wheels were beautiful, and its springy black leatherette seat was smart-looking. The fingertip-control brakes were handy, and so were the levers for controlling the rotation of the left and right wheels. Best of all, though, was a marvelous lightweight handle that allowed fine adjustment of the chair-back angle, over a range of 130 degrees.

And so, thanks to that wheelchair, we were unable to climb the stairs and instead went on deeper and deeper inside the labyrinth of the old hospital building.

To call it a labyrinth is neither a figure of speech nor an exaggeration. Units constructed gallery-style around a court-yard were joined together by corridors to form square wings, three units on a side, that were built around even larger court-yards. There were three such wings, laid out so that their adja-cent sides formed an equilateral triangle; the entire layout thus had all the complexity of three overlapping honeycombs. Furthermore, since sections of old-fashioned thick concrete and brick were mingled together, some parts had preserved their old structure while others had disintegrated and lay buried under heaps of earth and sand. Even if I had been familiar then with the overall layout of the place, I doubt if I could have told how I managed to arrive where I am now. If I were to start out today from that same underground passage, I would have no confidence whatever in my ability to find this place again.

That day, I began first of all by making sure of the most direct route to ground level, from an old lavatory up through a manhole. After that, whenever I had the chance I explored around a bit and tried to find other ways of getting in and out. Most of them were dead ends, forcing me to retrace my steps, and very few had any openings leading outside. Except for the terrible odor, like the smell of stuffed animals going bad, it seemed that I had finally stumbled on the ideal hideout. There weren't even any lice.

A couple of times, though, I had cause for alarm. Once was yesterday morning, when I went out to see the horse at the old firing practice range; while I was gone, the girl said she had heard voices through the wall. They were fairly loud, she said; one person just on the other side of the wall called to someone else far away, who gave a short answer, at which the person by the wall went off laughing derisively. But that's impossible. In the first place, there is no such thing as "the other side of the wall" in this room. I've checked it out carefully again and again so there's no doubt in my mind: except for the side with the door leading in and out, there is nothing beyond any of the walls except dirt and sand. At most there could only be a mole tunnel or two. She says flatly that the voices did not come from by the door, and I suppose I should believe her. That hall is wired with a three-way alarm system, anyway. So it must have been either a dream, a ringing in her ears, or a trick of the wind in the ventilator. I decided not to worry myself unnecessarily over it.

The second source of alarm is something that happened just now, while I was on my way back over the longest route, the one leading back from the animal cages by the museum. Fairly close to the hideout, I came upon a cigarette butt in the hallway. It had been rubbed out on something, and had about two centimeters left before the filter. Naturally, there was no trace of smoke, nor was it even hot to the touch. But what bothers me is that it was neither wet nor dried out, and that the whiteness of its paper seemed so fresh. Of course, mummies have been found looking as good as new, and a cigarette is a far simpler thing than a mummy, so maybe it's nothing to get excited about. Besides, the brand was Seven Stars, the same as mine, which is some reassurance. If it's something I did unconsciously, then no harm done; anyway, it's easier to assume that that's what happened. Let me see . . . how long ago did Seven Stars come out on the market?

Slowly, every so often, the ground began making howling noises.

5:02—

I removed the polythene bag I had stuffed into the ventilator and listened again. There it was, the noise of big drums. Evidently they were going to go ahead and follow the traditional forms. Refracted in the underground labyrinth, the reverberations roared like the ocean. Right about now the horse would be putting the scissors to the tape, to the accompaniment of light, scattered applause, his body stiffly erect above the waist.

Across that part of the evening sky visible through the ventilator hole move clouds like overboiled rice cakes. Blobby and swollen, they look as though at any moment they might burst open in a sudden gush of water.

The time is finally drawing near when we will have to leave this hideout. To keep these notes from getting wet I will put them inside a plastic bag, and seal the top firmly with cellophane tape. That crack in the wall shaped like a baseball cap will be a good place to hide the notebook. The brim-shaped part comes right out, and inside is an empty, pocket-like space.

I use it now as a safe in which to store cash, my railway pass, and the FM transmitter that I took from the chair leg in room eight.

In another thirty minutes I will wake up the girl.

From my point of view, it would actually be best to act alone as far as possible until I have gotten my wife safely back. At this point I have no idea what shape I may find her in, or under what conditions we may ever be able to meet again. It seems fairly certain that the pill thief had some connection with her disappearance, yet there's nothing to go on but circumstantial evidence. It could even be that I've only been made to think so by the horse's clever insinuations. Maybe my wife really was sick, and was hospitalized without being able to contact me for some minor reason. From her point of view, *I* would be the one who vanished without a trace that day. Or she might have taken a temporary job in the hospital library or somewhere, partly to track me down. Nor could I ignore the possibility that she lost her memory after being hit by the pill thief. In the worst event, she could be a captive somewhere, held forcibly through physical restraint, drugs, or hypnosis, deprived of free will.

In any case, I must take proper steps to deal with each of these possibilities. If necessary, I am even prepared to use violence. With the spring action of the jump shoes and this twenty-five-centimeter steel pipe I plan to carry under my arm, I should be able to achieve pretty good striking ability. The girl doesn't like jump shoes—she says just watching other people bound around makes her feel as though she's shrinking—so I'm a little rusty, but there is an innate reflex involved; it's not as though just anybody could jump with them on.

Having a wheelchair-ridden girl with me in that sort of situation will clearly put me at a disadvantage. If I'm not careful, we could both come to harm.

But the worse conditions become, the fewer chances there will be to come back to this hideout any more. I may have all I can do just to clear an escape route in order to smuggle my wife out of the hospital. To escape from there I would have to run downhill to the north, toward town—the opposite direction from here. If I leave the girl here when I go, then it means deserting her. I could resign myself one way or another if this notebook should end up forgotten in that crack in the wall, never to be seen by human eyes again. But the girl is different.

I packed a short supply of food in the trunk under the wheelchair.

Four bottles of Coke, five rolls, four croquettes, two cucumbers, two hard-boiled eggs, some salt wrapped in tin foil, a quarter of a pound of butter, a chocolate bar, four overripe peaches, some paper napkins . . .

The girl smiled, half opening her eyes, still wearing the radio earphones. One hand was stuck, as always, in her crotch. I have decided not to be too hard on her about that any more. No sooner did she smile at me than she was fast asleep again. Her body has gotten all out of shape. I keep changing her position to keep her from becoming too terribly misshapen (the Swedish wheelchair is well designed for that purpose, too), but no matter what I do, the more I touch her the rounder she becomes, like a rice cake or a lump of candy or a dumpling. Much as it galls me, I have to hand it to the horse for his skill as head of the cartilage surgery department.

Watching the girl become more and more infantile, I fall under the illusion that time is moving backward. But what she still has not lost is the expression in her eyes. If people are attracted to this girl, it must be because of those downward-tilting eyes, always gazing off so far in the distance that they cannot see what is right in front of them.

What to do with the uniform. It would be handy for blending in with the crowd, but also I have a feeling that it might become an easy target for pursuit. Since everything depends on the anniversary eve party, I finally decided that I might just as well take it along. Even if I don't use it myself, it might come in handy as a pillow for the girl.

What I hated most to leave behind was my sales briefcase.

It contained nothing of any particular value; only thirty jump shoe catalogues, fifteen order blanks, and fifteen bonus gift certificates. This may sound petty, but that briefcase is genuine Italian leather; I splurged on it more than I really should have. I know I should resign myself, but it's hard to see what I ever did to deserve such a loss.

6:07—

Time to go. The route is 8484332. That is the number of the route leading out by the museum, with the turns numerically encoded for easy remembrance.

"I dreamed about some rotten soap."

"Soap doesn't rot."

"Why not?"

"If it did, it wouldn't be soap."

Perhaps I should take the notebook along, after all. Rather than go to all the trouble of having someone else come and retrieve it for me after I'm outside the hospital, it is safer to contrive some way to carry it out myself. It will only be necessary when my back is to the wall anyway, so it makes more sense to keep it close by so that I can adapt myself to circumstances as they arise. I decided to insert it between the springs and the seat bottom in the back of the wheelchair. Barring some need to repair the wheelchair frame, nobody is likely to think of looking there.

Epilogue

I climbed up between artificial rocks, carrying the wheelchair in my arms, and saw that the square in front of the museum was already filled with spectator seats for the anniversary eve party.

"That's the museum. Look, on top, there's a flagpole."

"That's an antenna."

"It's a flagpole."

"Well, maybe they use it for both."

Suddenly a voice spoke from the shadow of a parked car.

"Whoever heard of a flagpole without a flag, on a holiday?"

Like instant adhesive, the voice fastened down the soles of my shoes and stuck to the wheels of the wheelchair. All my fighting spirit poured out of me, as though a barrel had split open. Unable to believe my ears, hoping against hope it was someone else, I turned warily around, only to have my fears confirmed: it was indeed the assistant director's secretary.

She stood with a slightly set smile on her face, carrying in one hand a tattered old department store shopping bag. Her light-brown blouse and cocoa-colored skirt, neither of which I had seen before, did a good job of sheathing her usual bared-fangs look.

"So you knew all about it."

"You get better-looking all the time."

"This is a life-and-death matter for us."

"I just saved you a lot of trouble. This is what you were after, isn't it?"

The secretary looked up at me, biting her lip, and took a layer of newspapers off the top of the shopping bag. A wad of spongy scarlet cloth was rolled up and stuffed inside. The girl turned as rigid as an infant having convulsions.

"I'm scared."

"Well, if you don't want it I'll just throw it away. After all the trouble I went to, smashing the showcase window and stealing it for you . . ."

Angrily the secretary lifted up the wad of cloth on the end of a stick she had picked up off the ground, and waved it around as hard as she could. It looked like the scarlet corpse of a cat run over by an automobile.

"Is that your mother, who had watafuki disease?"

"It's all stiff, like old felt. And it smells like mothballs; you can't use it without a gas mask."

Suddenly the girl clutched at the scarlet rag, stifling a scream. Then she moaned, choking with tears. The secretary stepped back, overpowered, and I felt a wave of jealousy at such strong emotion.

"She's happy."

"That's how nice I wanted you to be to me."

With the secretary's halfhearted assistance, I spread the quilt between the wheelchair and the girl. The scarlet quilt contrasted oddly with the functional beauty of the wheelchair. The girl grabbed both ends of the quilt, turned her head to one side and said in a nasal, teary voice, "It's just the smell of mothballs, so I guess it's okay, huh?"

I began to feel tired. I sat down on a stone step and shared a bottle of lukewarm Coke with the secretary. Absorbed in her quilt, the girl had no time to spare on a Coke. The secretary pressed a bare foot, sticking out from under her skirt, over against my leg.

"This is like a picnic!"

The sky was as black as an internal hemorrhage. It looked as though it might rain at any moment. I tossed the empty bottle into a clump of grass, and a woman screamed. Undaunted, the secretary screamed right back:

"Pipe down!"

It was a depressing start. If my plan had been discovered already, there was no chance of carrying it out. On the other hand, it was senseless to think of retreat.

We walked across the square in front of the museum and down the street by the park; soon the sidewalks became crowded with rows of concession stands smelling of acetylene gas. I decided to cut through the park by the side entrance;

inside, it was as deserted as before. White smoke filled the air, followed by the bang of promotional firecrackers.

"Looks like she's gone back to the shape she was in before she came to the hospital."

"Will it get any worse?"

"Depends on how long the tensile strength of her bones can withstand the pressure of her internal organs."

"What do you mean?"

"Just imagine what would happen to an umbrella if its spokes started to melt. You get the idea."

By the fountain in the park the electric-guitar band was still listlessly at practice, halfway through a rock number that sounded more like something for a Bon festival dance. A goldfish-scooping stand and a booth selling small pastry figurines were the only places open for business. Seated on a bench were a nurse (for some reason she had on her uniform cap) dressed in short shorts that revealed a shocking amount of thigh, and beside her a young one-legged boy with a black dog suffering from a skin disease. Their eyes were fastened on the spray of water in the fountain, watching as it twisted and breathed.

Drops splashed at my feet. A pink moth the size of a little bird flew into a puddle formed by windblown spray.

"It's cold."

The girl's shoulders were shaking. When I wrapped the scarlet quilt around her shoulders she looked like a stone statue of Jizō out on a country road, with a bib tied around its neck. My collar was sweaty.

We came back out onto the street through the main gate.

All at once, as though bursting from a paper festival ball, a great crowd of people began pouring out of nowhere. Halfway up a long slope was the entrance to a vast underground shopping district, which looked as though the steep hillside had been completely hollowed out. Printed in huge letters across an arch rimmed with neon lights was a sign that read: CON-GRATULATIONS—HOSPITAL FOUNDING DAY—PLEASANTVIEW GINZA STREET. The girl fluttered her hands and cried out excitedly.

Hundreds of abandoned bicycles lay scattered everywhere, and all kinds of people were milling around expectantly: office workers, young people in blue jeans, doctors and nurses in uniform, even patients still in pajamas, who looked as if they had escaped from their rooms only moments before. It didn't look like any ordinary street.

Was this the site of the anniversary eve party, then?

"Pleasantview—what a name for an underground plaza!"

"It's the real name of this place. Supposedly when you climb up on top you can see Mount Fuji."

"Isn't this dangerous? If they dug in just a little farther they'd undermine the old hospital foundations."

"What do you mean? Foundations are the lowest part, by definition."

"This underground plaza must go lower than that, though, doesn't it?"

"You still don't have the picture, do you? That place where you were hiding out was on the third floor of the old building."

"No, you're kidding."

"The old director had all the hospital buildings built underground. He had a thing about bomb raids or something."

Drop by drop, big, heavy raindrops began to pelt the earth. The girl opened her mouth to taste them, and spoke in an affected singsong—it may actually have been part of the lyrics of some song: "No matter how bad the weather, in my memory it's always a beautiful day...."

Pushed by the crowd, which was beginning to move underground to escape the rain, we too passed beneath the neon arch. The underground mall was at first like any normal street, lined on either side with decorative streetlights. This also appeared to be part of the hospital grounds: florists, fruit stores, bedding stores, and handicraft shops were everywhere, with shoe stores, optical goods stores, bookshops, toyshops, drugstores, bakeries, stationery stores, noodle shops, and cigarette stands sandwiched in between. Gradually the way grew narrower, branching off irregularly again and again, leading us on in farther and farther. Along the way we encountered stairs that gave us some trouble, but we pushed heedlessly ahead. The girl was excited and in high spirits, showing no particular signs of discomfort; even the secretary had for once adjusted her step to mine.

The stores slowly changed in character as we walked along.

An automobile accessories store, a jeans specialty shop, a wholesale dealer in Chinese medicinal herbs, a record store, and an electrical appliances discount store; a pinball parlor offering all the Coke you could drink, out of which blared a rousing military song; a barbecued chicken stand, around which empty beer bottles littered the street; a camera store where photos were developed and printed; a lending library; a curried rice and salad restaurant; a store that specialized in bugging equipment; an ice cream stand. . . .

I bought three chocolate cones at the stand. The girl, still clinging to the quilt in one hand, stuck her tongue into the ice cream with a dreamy look. It tasted sad, as though time itself were starting to freeze over.

Beyond the next narrow cross street was a public lavatory, past which the area changed complexion entirely: neon lights danced on provocative signs as game corners, cabarets, and strip joints jostled for space. It was not a very fitting place to stroll pushing a little girl in a wheelchair, accompanied by a female secretary. I felt some hesitation. Something up ahead, though, aroused my sense of smell. If I was ever to encounter my wife again, this might be my only chance. Though I had nothing much to base it on, a presentiment very like confidence was ringing an alarm bell, telling me I was near my goal.

If only I could leave the wheelchair with the secretary and go on alone, that would be perfect.

"Do you suppose it's safe to trust you with something?"

"Why, sure; if you trust me, I'll act like I'm being trusted."

"If you keep your promise, then what shall I do for you?"

"Better think of something yourself."

I could see her pupils contract, seared by a flash of anger that seemed to run between her temples like electricity through a tube. However much I decided to trust her, it could only be for the length of time it took them to finish their ice cream cones, at most. I couldn't bring myself to leave the girl in her keeping any longer than that.

All of a sudden the girl cried out.

"It's the doctor—look, over there. . . ."

The tip of her ice cream cone was pointed diagonally across the street at a building that looked like a real estate office. A sign the width of the window frame announced in gold cutout letters: ALL INTERNAL ORGANS BOUGHT AND SOLD. Underneath it, the glass was crowded with a variety of other signs, each with a price list: BLOOD COLLECTION CENTER, SPERM BANK, CORNEA INSURANCE, and the like. On the door an inconspicuous wooden sign was marked: RECREATION INFORMATION BUREAU.

Peering through the narrow spaces between price lists, I could barely make out parts of the store inside. When I brought my eyes down to the level of the girl's, the spaces seemed larger; by squinting alternately through my right and left eyes, I found the parts became a decipherable mosaic. By the window was a circular table where seven or eight white-coated doctors sat drinking beer. One was rocking back and forth, stroking the stubble on his chin; another was laughing like a hyena, showing an unseemly amount of teeth, while another scraped the bowl of his pipe with a matchstick. Each seemed absorbed in his own pursuits, in an atmosphere of comfortable relaxation. Some of them might have been women, but I could not tell for certain. In the rear of the store was a counter where another man in white stood conversing with a woman, his spine held unnaturally straight. The woman behind the counter had a broad forehead and wore rimless glasses; her low-cut blouse emphasized her buxomness. She looked exactly like Kei Mano from the Mano Agency in front of the hospital. Then would that fellow with the ramrod back be the assistant director?

The cone in my hand fell apart like wet bread. I tossed the rest of it under the wheelchair and licked the ice cream off my fingers. Glancing over at the secretary, I saw that she too was squatting down and peering intently into the store.

"Is that the assistant director?"

"Yes. The others are staff doctors from the artificial organs department, I think."

"What do you think would happen if they saw us here?"

Nibbling on the edge of her cone, the girl said in a low voice, "I bet he'd give me a real scolding."

"Well, he hasn't got the right. Who gave him the right to do a thing like that?"

The secretary said nothing. She continued to watch, as though busily calculating how best to deal with the situation. Undoubtedly she knew exactly what was going on: what they were doing there, and what they would be up to next. Even I had a vague inkling, so there was no reason the assistant director's private secretary wouldn't know all about it. She was only keeping still while she weighed the pros and cons of letting me in on the secret.

"Let's go back." As though our tension had communicated itself, the girl spoke up in a frightened voice.

"Back where?"

"Anywhere."

Stroking her cheek, I rubbed the sleep from her eyes. My fingers had a lingering sensation of being covered with soft, dry starch.

The secretary stood up hurriedly and looked around.

"As long as they don't catch sight of us, nothing in particular should come of it."

So at last she had decided to become my ally. Inside the store, the men were starting to get up from their chairs. I hid us in the shadow of a pillar, wheelchair and all, and ordered again; this time everybody had orange sherbet.

There were seven doctors including the assistant director. Sent off by the cheery farewells of the woman resembling Kei Mano, they hurried across the street and disappeared together inside the public lavatory.

Even after some time had passed, none of them reappeared. My sherbet was half gone. This long a stay could mean one thing only: they were taking a crap. But for seven men to have to crap together all at the same time was a little too coincidental. Besides, the assistant director, with his rubber corset, wasn't supposed to be able to use an ordinary john. Maybe something unusual had come up. I decided to wait another two minutes—no, one: then if they still hadn't come out, I would barge my way in.

Leaving the secretary and the girl behind, I looked inside. Beneath an out-of-order sign hung a board on which was faintly visible the word MEN. Not a soul was in sight. In all the too-bright fluorescent light and foul ammonia stench I could see no shadows that might have concealed seven men. Six discolored urinals were lined up along the left wall. The first was filled with a yellow liquid in which a bug was swimming around and around, clinging to a bubble. On the opposite wall were three stalls done in brand-new paneling, perhaps set up especially for that night. I could hardly suppose two or three men were herded inside each stall, but just to make certain I knocked on each one in turn, opening the doors and checking inside. All were empty.

The last one, however, was different. Instead of a toilet bowl it had a square opening with stairs that led down to a dim underground room. In the ceiling was another opening with a steel ladder, like a hatch leading up to the deck of a cargo ship. That explained how they had disappeared; they must have gone either up or down. But I could not detect a single clue. It would have taken considerable time for all seven men to pass through; I regretted again not having come in sooner. Nobody needs an excuse to enter a public john.

As I was leaving I stumbled into someone who immediately began yelling at me.

"What's the matter, can't you read? The sign says out of order."

It was the woman from the information bureau. She studied me appraisingly; undaunted, I gave her an appraising look of my own. Out of order, my ass. With my own eyes I had seen her waving them off. There was no point in getting into an argument, though. I needed to find out from her which way they had gone.

"Aren't you Miss Mano from the agency?"

Far from warming to me, she only deepened the wrinkles

in her forehead in greater suspicion and said, "I've seen you someplace. Was it at the store in front of the hospital?"

The secretary, who had followed with the wheelchair, now spoke up on my behalf.

"This is the new chief of security."

The woman's reaction was swift; I remembered then having been told that all the agencies across from the hospital were under the direct supervision of the chief of security. She smiled awkwardly with her upper lip, rising to the occasion.

"Tickets have been selling very well, I'm glad to say, even though the odds aren't too favorable. We're completely sold out. So you're the new chief, are you? Well, that's nice. Just a minute or two ago the assistant director and six other young doctors bought up all the rest of the tickets and . . ."

"Where'd they go?"

"You mean you don't know?"

"Just answer the question, please."

"Certainly."

"Upstairs or down?"

"There's nothing downstairs but a machine room. Surely . . ."

"Thanks."

The secretary hung back, claiming that she couldn't bring herself to set foot inside a men's toilet. She wouldn't listen to the argument that it was out of order anyway, but finally I managed to persuade her by taking the steel pipe and scraping off the remnants of the word MEN from the sign.

The secretary climbed up the ladder first, and I passed the girl up to her. Then I followed with the wheelchair on my shoulders. It didn't weigh too much, but it was too big to go through the opening that way. I had to rest one set of wheels on the edge and keep it balanced while I pushed it up with my head.

In the midst of all this, the girl started to cry. It was a stifled sobbing, as though she were in pain. The secretary sought confusedly to comfort her. Busy struggling with the wheelchair, I was unable to tell which of them was antagonizing which. I decided not to make matters worse. The best solution would be to make sure that they were not left alone together again.

The corridor was cool, and smelled of earth. The rooms on either side were boarded up; there was no sign of life. Roughly every ten meters or so hung a naked twenty-watt bulb, and that was all. Every corner, however, was marked with an arrow made of red vinyl tape, and it seemed likely that by following those we would eventually arrive somewhere. Besides, after four days in the hideout I had a fairly good idea of the overall building plan by then.

The floor sucked up the noise of our footsteps like dry clay. It was as if we had rubber plugs in our ears. When we spoke, our voices echoed as if we were in the bottom of a well, so we ended up speaking in whispers.

"You know what this is all about, don't you?"

"Yes, more or less."

"What's going on?" Even the girl had lowered her voice.

"What difference does it make?" The secretary cut her off nervously. "Our business will be over soon enough."

We walked on, turned a corner at an odd angle, and seemed to enter a different wing. All of a sudden the murmur of voices grew louder and the hallway brightened; the area was thronged with people. Each wing in the building consisted of nine smaller divisions, each surrounding a courtyard, that contained six rooms apiece. This division was filled with a good-sized crowd of spectators who were circling around meekly clockwise, as at an exhibition. Since we hadn't seen anyone else along the way, that must have been a special route for authorized personnel only.

An announcement was being made in a tone so monotonous that it reminded me of a science news reporter.

Of the six contestants who passed the preliminary match, the two in the top group are still . . . has already completed twenty-nine steps . . . just now six times, maintaining an average of nine or above, and a total of one hundred and fourteen seconds . . . not showing . . . inserting a chilled rod, three

minutes . . . installed with a warranty from the medical society
of . . . comparing these data with a computer forecast graph,
the difference is again . . .

Mingling in with the crowd, we decided to go around
once. There were a few female spectators, though not many;
hardly surprisingly, we saw no one with children.

In each room hung a bulletin board displaying a photograph of a nude woman; those would be photographs of the
contestants. Various numbers were posted magnetically next to
the photos. In some places the postings were being changed. I
couldn't figure out what they meant. Over the doors were bizarre names like DOLL PAVILION, TIDAL WAVE WOMAN, MAGMA,
and SWAN LAKE, all written in big, brightly colored letters.
Probably they were contestants' code names. Most of the spectators held a folded tabloid-style newspaper in one hand, in
which they made notes as they compared its listings with the
posted code names and numbers. The atmosphere was exactly
like that at a bicycle-racing stadium.

Around the corner from Tidal Wave Woman and directly
across from Magma was a lounge selling food and drinks,
crowded full of people. At a table in the middle sat six white-
coated doctors, munching on potato chips and sipping on what
appeared to be Scotch and water. No other clusters of men in
white were to be seen, so they had to be the assistant director's
companions. The assistant director himself would not be able to
sit down because of his corset; probably he had mixed in with
the crowd at the counter.

Taking advantage of the throng, we hastily slipped on by.

At the next corner was Masked Woman. As the name
suggested, her face had been painted in a white mask. The color
was no ordinary white, however, but a soft, pearly luster of
such exquisite quality that it seemed to liquidate all facial expression. Apparently she was especially popular; the crowd
there was quite dense.

"Isn't that your wife?"

The possibility had suggested itself to me, but I could not
be sure. Or rather, if I could move on past without admitting
that possibility, then that was what I wanted to do. There was

one more room. Quickly rounding the corner, we came to Fire-eating Bird. The photograph on the bulletin board was of someone entirely different. Then had Masked Woman been my wife after all? I was attacked by a horrid sensation, as if myriad baby spiders were crawling out of pores all over my body. I had thought that I was prepared, but no amount of mental resolve is equal to the shock of reality.

I decided to go around once more.

Doll Pavilion . . . Tidal Wave Woman . . . Magma . . . Swan Lake . . . none of those could have been my wife. Then for the second time, Masked Woman . . . again I thought to myself what a beautifully well-proportioned body she had. She did look a great deal like my wife. But if it was really she, then just a glimpse from behind ought to be sufficient to be sure. What could be the reason for this vague uncertainty?

"If there isn't anyone else, then she must be the one, right?"

Perhaps so. But there was no hard proof that my wife was actually among these able-bodied six, all winners of the preliminary match, to begin with. I was only trying to anticipate the worst.

"That's odd. Having to think so much to decide if someone is your own wife . . ."

Probably it did seem odd. But a man's wife always exists for him in the totality of her personality. However beautiful, what that photograph showed was nothing but an exquisite assemblage of various bodily parts. It was impossible to make any mental connection between that and my image of my wife. Besides, that thick layer of pearly white was sending the blood of a stranger coursing to the farthest reaches of her body. No doubt her personality had been utterly transformed, too.

"Well, well, all three of you together; isn't this unusual! Say, did you finish going over that manuscript for me?"

All at once the assistant director was standing directly behind us. The secretary stiffened automatically, but she did not seem particularly surprised.

"I typed up your speech for tomorrow in duplicate and gave one copy to the council. . . . Five Xerox copies will be enough, don't you think?"

"Plenty."

Were they fellow conspirators after all? The girl looked up at the assistant director with a helpless giggle. I felt betrayed. It had all come about so naturally that I got off to a bad start, and was unable to think of even one of the itemized questions that I had so carefully prepared for our next encounter.

"I would appreciate it if there were some way of checking out the real names of these contestants."

"Yeah. They sure came up with some far-out stage names, didn't they? Whoever's in charge around here must be into either Turkish baths or modern poetry, one of the two." Abruptly he gave the girl's ear a pinch and said in a sober voice, "Poor kid, look at the shape you're in."

The crowd of spectators parted and a trio of shaven-headed fellows in sweat pants appeared, running with the distinctive way of holding the knees that comes from wearing jump shoes. When they saw us, all three put their hands up by their temples, palms out, and flapped them like elephant ears. The assistant director addressed one of them, who was carrying some newspapers in a paper bag slung around his shoulder.

"Let me have one of those, will you?"

"Can't, sir; these are tomorrow's papers."

The trio ran off, and the flow of onlookers returned to normal.

"You seem pretty interested in one of these women."

The secretary answered for me.

"He says she might be his wife."

"I see. . . ." The assistant director glanced at the photograph on the bulletin board and gave a wry smile. "Still, you are keeping up with the notebooks, I hear."

"What do you mean, 'still'?"

"I suppose I mean something like 'nevertheless.' Well, what do you say, shall we have a look inside? I've got some extra tickets, so there's one for you. I'm rather interested in this Masked Woman myself." He turned and addressed the secretary. "You take the girl and go down to the lounge for a coffee or something, okay?"

The secretary bore down hard on the instep of my jump shoe with all her weight.

"I'm only waiting five minutes, hear? Keep an eye on the clock. I was going to have you touch me real nice. I'm entitled to that much."

From inside the wheelchair as the secretary pushed it farther and farther away, the girl gazed back with an imploring look. I couldn't tell which of us she was looking at. Not only were her eyes far away, but she seemed to be squinting slightly besides. I wiped away tears. They were from the pain in my foot, but the assistant director seemed to misunderstand.

"Now, I'm not going to jump on you for anything right now. But sometimes a little cruelty is necessary. Doctors are cruel, and patients endure their cruelty . . . that's the law of survival."

We pushed our way through a throng of people, all of whom stared resentfully at the tickets in our hands, and went through the door marked MASKED WOMAN. Inside was a reception area surrounded on all four sides by black cloth. When one layer was pushed aside, another appeared in its place. Pushing right and left through layer after layer of cloth (for the life of me, I could not tell what order they went in), finally we came to a white-tiled room that looked like a lecture amphitheater for a dissection. In the front of the room was a semicircular cylinder covered with curved mirrors, surrounded fanwise by rows of nearly full seats.

A dry, expressionless voice came over the speakers.

The three-minute intermission will soon be over. Please take your seats.

Since of course the assistant director could not sit down, I decided to join him standing up.

The houselights dimmed and the cylindrical mirrors vanished; in their place appeared a wide bed. Evidently they were two-way mirrors. On the bed was a naked woman, her face painted white exactly as advertised, lying with her feet pointed toward the audience. Shudders began to spread outward from the core of my body like ripples of water. To keep the assistant director from noticing, I held my body stiff, but then my back teeth began to rattle like an old washing machine.

"Well? Isn't she something? She may look a little delicate, but they say she's got such a big lead now on the runner-up, Doll Pavilion, that she has the championship all wrapped up."

Inserted between the woman's legs, which were half parted with one knee raised, was some sort of metal apparatus attached to a cord. Electrodes taped to her knees, hips, and shoulders were connected by fine insulated wires to a machine by the bed. Even in that state she had beauty and charm, rather like a dancer in the role of a captive Martian.

Two doctors in lab coats came out from in back, removed the apparatus from between her legs, and inspected the machine. With an air of familiarity, one of them gave her nipples a casual pinch and murmured words of encouragement as he left. The woman jerked reflexively.

"Amazing, isn't it. She stays just on the verge of an orgasm."

"Can she be cured?"

"If it's a sickness, it's a disease afflicting patients that stems from what you might call personality forfeiture, so it's untreatable; treatment isn't considered necessary anyway."

"That's horrible."

"Is she really your wife?"

"For some reason I'm just not sure. . . ."

"Some help you are. Speaking of your wife, by the way . . . the sex psychologists say she was suffering from a form of rape delusion."

"Did you find her?"

"Remember that tape we listened to together, the one made in the outpatient waiting room? That noise like a sack of starch falling over evidently was your wife falling down, after all. She had a mild brain concussion. When she came to, she suddenly found herself surrounded by a circle of white-masked men. As a matter of fact, it was nothing but an ordinary examining room, but your wife jumped to the conclusion that she was going to be gang-raped. Rape delusion, you see, is a defensive arousal mechanism for escaping from the fear of rape. Fighting fire with fire, you might say. In other words, it's a kind of compensatory arousal."

"What bullshit!"

"You've gotten awfully sure of yourself, haven't you?" The assistant director arched his back and looked over one shoulder at me like a comical camel, alternately stretching out and screwing up his upper lip. "Never mind; while the cat was away you certainly managed to get in your share of playing, didn't you? Holing up somewhere with the girl from room eight and carrying on with her from morning till night . . ."

"We were not 'carrying on'!"

"You don't have to yell!" He was the one who was yelling. Several people turned around and gave us dirty looks. "Do whatever you want with her. Have her boiled or fried, just as you like. Of course, I'd be fooling myself if I said I didn't miss her. You're right, she was as nice as freshly squeezed orange juice . . . but I've decided to get over her once and for all. With the champion of tonight's contest . . . the orgasm record-holder and the horse-man . . . that combination should make it considerably easier to get my idea across to people, don't you think? Give me your opinion. I've asked two or three people and so far everyone agrees with me. . . ."

"I don't know the first thing about any idea of yours."

"That's impossible. It's all set up for tomorrow's festival. After the memorial address, as horse-man I'm going to have intercourse in front of all the participants. With the winner of tonight's contest. The idea is to give a personal demonstration of the ultimate retrogression, myself."

"Playing monster, is that it?"

"You sure like to give a guy a hard time. When will you ever accept the true ugliness of health? If animal history has been a history of evolution, then the history of mankind is one of retrogression. Hooray for monsters! Monsters are the great embodiments of the weak."

A buzzer sounded. A blue "Ready" light faded and a red "On" light took its place. Led out by a large, dark nurse, a balding, plump, middle-aged man came out timidly from the side door. A mane of pubic hair billowed around his erect penis, which he shyly covered with both hands. When the nurse pulled his hands away, the organ began losing its vitality before our eyes.

The assistant director clucked his tongue lightly.

"No good; he's too nervous."

The nurse rubbed oil on the middle-aged man's penis and gave it an encouraging squeeze-pull. It regained its luster, and the audience roared approval. The woman parted her thighs at a signal, and the nurse injected some sort of fluid into the nicotine-colored place in her crotch, using an enema syringe. It was probably some sort of lubricating oil. A series of convulsions ran like ripples in a water bed from the woman's abdominal region up under her ribs.

"You must have some way of finding out just who this woman is and where she's from."

"You aren't exactly in a position to go around talking that way any more, are you?"

The middle-aged man crawled up on the bed, his round bottom toward us, and knelt between her legs. The woman twisted her head to the right, both fists tightly clenched. The move did have a familiar look, but I couldn't be certain. The man was awkwardly shifting the position of his hips and bending his head; then, without changing posture, he started to masturbate. Evidently his penis had gone completely down. Laughter burst out from the audience, and even the woman lifted up her head to peer between his legs.

"If I could only see her closer up, then I'm sure I'd be able to tell. . . ."

"That's it! You do it!" The assistant director spoke suddenly, choking on his laughter. "With luck, your body will remember for you!"

The nurse came out with a syringe and gave the middle-aged man a quick shot in one buttock, then swabbed the site of the injection with alcohol-soaked cotton. Already, though, the attention of the audience had focused on me. A man with a plaster cast around his neck sitting in front of us turned around, grabbed my cock, and yelled, "It's up! He's rarin' to go!"

"Watch it, buddy."

The assistant director gave me a shove down to the end of the aisle. The steps, which were made of stainless-steel pipes, were about forty centimeters apart. If I ever lost my footing, it would be all I could do to stay upright. Somebody yanked on my shirttail, and a button popped off. The only way to keep from falling down headfirst was to go on down the stairs without trying to resist. My belt came off. My shirt sleeves were ripped to shreds. My fly came unzipped, and my pants slid down around my feet. By the time I had finally reached the bottom of the stairs and recovered my balance, I was dressed absurdly in nothing but my shorts, my jump shoes, and the back of my shirt. Lewd howls and war whoops flew back and forth in the hall, and seemed to penetrate even inside the two-way mirror. The woman propped herself up on one elbow, craned her white neck, and looked out from between the middle-aged man's legs to see what was happening outside. The nurse sent flustered signals backstage, and the lighting dimmed until the glass cylinder reverted to being a mirror once again. Now it was our turn to be seen. Had she recognized me? . . .

I turned my back to the mirrors, took the steel pipe out from under my arm, and steadied myself. Then, holding it aloft menacingly in the air, I started back up the stairs. The five minutes I had promised the secretary were almost up. All I had to do was go and explain the situation to her, and then come back again. Even as I told myself that, however, I was well aware that in part it was only an excuse. I might just as easily have smashed the two-way mirror and forced my way inside. Instead I had chosen to back down. It made no sense even to me. Or was I just trying not to understand?

Several times I encountered heavy resistance, and heard screams. Brandishing the steel pipe, I ran inside the area partitioned with black cloth.

Inside was nothing but a dim light reflected off the ceiling; I could just barely make out my hand ahead of me in the dark. To keep from being taken by surprise, I stabbed and beat at the cloths with my pipe as I went. No one seemed to be after me, but the path was far more intricate than I had dreamed. In a series of two-meter-square enclosures, the way would be now straight ahead, now on one side; it was an endless maze, with no seeming pattern in all the turns and twists. Realizing that the assistant director had led us through in less than a minute only made me more impatient, which threw my sense of direction all the farther off track.

Suddenly, weaving through the black cloth walls like a howling wind, there came the echo of a woman's deep, sad moaning. It sounded like the cry the north wind makes on clear winter evenings, brushing against telephone wires. Had the injection helped that middle-aged man to recover? Or had some other man taken his place? Swathed head to foot in black cloth, I kept pushing blindly ahead, frantically thrusting curtains aside one after another. Whether it meant that I would escape from my wife or be pulled back to her, I didn't care. Abruptly the voices receded, and I stepped outside the door.

Out in the hall it was as crowded as ever. Everyone who had not been able to purchase a ticket stared at me inquisitively. I had come bursting out of the very place they were all dying to see, my eyes bloodshot and nothing on but a pair of shorts. Naturally they were suspicious. Quietly I laid the steel pipe down on the floor, put my hands on my hips and decided to keep running, against the flow of the crowd. With luck they might assume I was just out jogging.

The lounge had begun to empty a little, but there was no sign of the secretary. Looking at my watch, I saw that it was thirty minutes past the time we had agreed on. Had she given up waiting and gone off somewhere? Using my jump shoes, I leaped up nearly to the ceiling. On the third try I caught a glimpse of someone in a light-tan blouse crouching down in a far corner. No, she wasn't crouching down; she was sitting in the wheelchair reading a newspaper. I felt an ugly premonition. I jumped up again, but there was no sign of the girl from room eight. In revenge for my broken promise she might have thrown her away, or given her to someone else. Ignoring the curses hurled my way, I scrambled madly through the crowd, cutting straight across the room. When the secretary saw me, she looked me up and down as if stifling an urge to laugh, then calmly offered me the newspaper she was reading.

"Look, this is tomorrow's paper."

Between the scarlet quilt and the secretary's bottom, a reddish putty-like substance was poking out. She was sitting on top of the girl. Overwhelmed by an emotion that was neither rage nor pain, I grabbed the secretary's arm and wrenched her up with all my might. With a sound of popping joints she rose in the air and landed under a nearby table with an exaggerated scream. When I lifted up the girl in the wheelchair, she squirmed slightly and groaned. Her life appeared to be in no immediate danger. Taking hold of what I guessed were her hands and feet, I pulled on them gently. I had a feeling that if I nursed her awhile, eventually I could have her back looking like a human being again.

Suddenly three young men in sweat pants appeared out of the crowd. One offered an arm to the secretary, and another sidled toward me in a karate stance. The third came at me silently with his fists, from the side. I twisted narrowly out of range and exchanged blows with him; in the instant when I attempted to lay the girl back in her wheelchair, the man in front came charging at me, head down. I barely managed to swallow a violent impulse to retch before I felt my consciousness plunge into a sea of nausea. Faces of bystanders surrounding me at a distance were as red as gladioli. Just before I was shut up inside a rubber bag, thicker than the assistant director's corset, I heard the voice of the secretary singing far away.

Say the multiplication table.

Someone began reading a memorial address for me.

Two times two is four, two times three is six, two times four is eight, two times five is ten . . .

I came to in the dark. After groping around awhile, I found the wheel of the wheelchair and finally remembered what had happened. A dull pain lingered beneath my ribs. Rubbing my stomach, I opened the trunk under the wheelchair, took out a flashlight, and checked on the girl. She was as oddly distorted as a rubber doll blown up too hard, but putting my ear up close, I could hear faint breathing. In the depths of my irrational joy at being alone with her at last, my eyes filled with tears. I stuck a finger in the crease under her jaw and rubbed gently. She half opened her eyes, blinking as though the light were dazzling. I kissed her nipples, which were like two scars. An answering sound met my ears, as though someone had stepped on a ball with a hole in it.

I explored the room with the flashlight. The chairs, the tables, the counter, the piles of empty bottles and paper cups, all had disappeared without a trace. The floor was buried in a thick layer of ancient dust, undisturbed by a single footprint. I began to wonder if last night's celebration had not been a festival of ghosts. Everything about the building itself was as I remembered it, though. The girl lay crushed in the wheelchair, and on my stomach was clearly imprinted the shape of that man's head. What's more, next to the wheelchair, "tomorrow's newspaper" lay crumpled where it had been tossed.

I listened. Everywhere, always, there was utter silence, not a sign of life stirring.

I thought I might leave the girl and go over for a look around the contest site. But if when I came back she and the wheelchair had disappeared like everything else, then there was no point in going. I touched her, and she felt dry and powdery. As if molding her out of clay, I tried pinching her here and there; after a time it did seem she had regained some bit of humanness. She was whispering something. I bent my ear down close to the apparent source of her voice.

"Touch me. . . ."

Layers of skin and muscle hung so slackly around her melted bones that I was unable to tell with any certainty which crease was her groin. I kept fondling her, touching every wrinkle I could find. Her breath started coming faster, her whole body grew moist, and finally she fell asleep.

Smoothing out "tomorrow's newspaper," I spread it out on the floor. The lead story contained a graphic description, filled with all manner of details, of the passionate mating between the horse-man with two penises and Masked Woman, holder of the orgasm record. The horse-man had tried to use both his penises, but had run into difficulty because of the corset. Finally he had made do just with his extra one. Nevertheless, everyone who watched the performance had been strongly impressed. The reporter's name, in parentheses, was "(Horse)."

I find it impossible, however, to accept such a thing as a past which has not yet begun.

I started to walk, pushing the wheelchair. I knew my way around the building fairly well. It had to be the second floor we were on, so all I needed to do was find a passage leading either up or down. The stairs all seemed to have crumbled and fallen, so my only hope was that hatchway in that lavatory. I kept on walking. As I walked I drew a map in my head, alternately drawing lines and erasing them. There should have been one lavatory in every section, but for some reason I rarely came across any. When I did find one every once in a while, everything was always firmly fastened down. There was never even enough room to poke an arm through.

Dozens of hours went by, and the beam from my flashlight began to weaken. My original optimism began changing to a breathless fear, as though I were rolling down a steep hill. I inserted the batteries in the listening device and tried calling, covertly at first. Speaking to no one in particular, I asked casually for directions.

When I grew tired I took the batteries out and inconspicuously embraced the girl. Sometimes I would have an erection myself. The girl's wrinkles grew deeper and deeper, and she seemed to recede farther and farther from human shape.

Finally the flashlight batteries went dead. I turned to the listening device and began to scream, abandoning all pride. It was the horse I called to. I admitted that I was sick, and swore over and over in as loud a voice as I could muster that I would be a perfect patient.

I can no longer see my watch, so I do not know how many days have gone by. Our provisions have run out, and so has our supply of drinking water. Even so, whenever I grow tired I take out the batteries and put my arms around the girl. She hardly ever responds any more. One of these times the batteries in the listening device will go dead, too, and then I will be able to go on holding her without fear of anyone.

I gnaw on the quilt made of the girl's mother and lick drops of water oozing from the concrete walls, clinging tightly to this secret rendezvous for one that no one can begrudge me now. However much I may resent the fact, "tomorrow's newspaper" has stolen a march on me; and so, in the past called tomorrow, over and over I continue certainly to die.

Embracing a tender, secret rendezvous for one . . .

A Note About the Author

Kobo Abe was born in Tokyo, but grew up in Mukden, Manchuria, where his father, a doctor, was on the staff of the medical school. At the end of World War II he returned to Japan. In 1948 he received a medical degree from Tokyo Imperial University, but he has never practiced medicine. In that same year he published his first book, *The Road Sign at the End of the Street*, and three years later he received the most important Japanese literary award, the Akutagawa Prize, for his novella *The Crime of Mr. S. Karuma*. In 1960 his novel *The Woman in the Dunes* won the Yomiuri Prize for Literature; subsequently this book was made into a film, which won the Jury Prize at the Cannes Film Festival, and it became the first of Mr. Abe's novels to be published in translation in the United States. Among his other major works which have been translated into English and other languages are *The Box Man*, *The Ruined Map*, *The Face of Another*, and *Inter Ice Age 4*. Today, Kobo Abe directs his own theater company in Tokyo, for which he creates several new plays each year. The company toured the United States in the summer of 1979, presenting performances in several cities. Mr. Abe lives in Tokyo with his wife, the artist and stage designer Machi Abe.